FANTASY
ROOMS

FANTASY ROOMS

INSPIRATIONAL DESIGNS FROM THE BBC SERIES

LAURENCE LLEWELYN-BOWEN

BOXTREE

DEDICATION

For my lionesses

Published in 1999 by Boxtree, an imprint of Macmillan Publishers Ltd,
25 Eccleston Place, London, SW1W 9NF and Basingstoke

Associated companies throughout the world

Fantasy Rooms is produced by Bazal for the BBC

ISBN 0 7522 1487 X

Text copyright © BBC and Bazal

Illustrations by Laurence Llewelyn-Bowen

The right of Laurence Llewelyn-Bowen to be identified as the author of this work has
been asserted by him in accordance with the Copyright, Designs and Patents Act 1988.

All photographs by Paul Bricknell, copyright © Boxtree, except for: photographs on
pages 11, 13, 72, 73, 101, 102, 155, 156, 159 which were supplied by ET archive; pages
130 (Tim Street-Porter), 131 (Tim Street-Porter), 133 which were supplied by Elizabeth
Whiting & Associates; pages 1, 4, 18, 45, 76, 106,134, 160, 192 which were
photographed by Nicky Johnston/OK! magazine; pages 20, 47, 79, 111, 137, 163 which
were photographed by Jonathan Martin;
and pages 39 and 43 which were supplied by the Ritz.

Cover photographs: front cover and black flap by Nicky Johnston/OK! magazine,
all others by Paul Bricknell

9 8 7 6 5 4 3 2 1 (or if centered 1 3 5 7 9 8 6 4 2)

A CIP catalogue record for this book is available from the British Library

Design by DW Design London

Printed by Milanostampa/ New Interlitho

CONTENTS

INTRODUCTION

It's odd, you know. If I granted you access to my fantasy, you'd be surprised. My fantasy room is the bedroom of a Holiday Inn *circa* 1974. We're talking about an interior that is so far removed from design, so divorced from style, it's not true. My fantasy is being able to escape from Planet Design for a few hours. When you enter an interior which has brown needlecord carpet on the ceiling, you know you can really switch off your aesthetic antennae.

I've had a riot making this television series. I've loved meeting people who really don't care what the neighbours think. The Brits are appalling at letting their hair down – OK, it's not really something you can do at work without either annoying or turning on the boss. But honestly, when the front door is shut, why not be who you really want to be? Don't dream it, live it. If the fantasy fits, wear it.

Home alone is your perfect excuse to be what you feel is you. We really can't change much of life, but there are a few areas where we can assert ourselves and right the wrongs that happen during the week, that redress the balance and turn us into the us we know we really are. Believe it or not, interior design is one.

It's because it's interior, it's because it's inside; because it's something we can enjoy and we can choose to share with a select group of friends. Forget estate agents – if you're worrying about selling your home in the future and use it as an excuse to deny the real you, how many more trivial roadblocks are you prepared to throw up in the way of your own real expression? Chances are a photograph in an estate agent's window that shows an interior completely conceived around your own specific fantasy will find a comparable fantatic with the cash to buy your property. Hey, you might even get a hot date out of it.

There is no excuse to hold back these days. It's not as if you actually have to give money to an overpaid, overcuffed, overcoiffed society designer physically to come round and measure up your living room. There is enough information to inspire you, enough to tell you how, and the product is getting increasingly easy to use – so go and use it. I hope that the television series, and this book, demonstrate how other people have had the commitment to express themselves no matter where they live. I feel privileged to help them, but what really interests me are the fantasies that have been reflected in interior design schemes up and down the country, designed, conceived and executed by true fantasy lovers, without me there to hold their hands.

I thought you'd be amused to see what really goes on. Planet Television makes everyone in the series look so good, so unreachable. The reality is much more straightforward. At the end of the day I have an interior to finish and a fantasy to make solid – it gets sweaty, it gets complicated, sometimes it gets fraught. Thank goodness for the backstage helpers such as my invaluable handyman Frank the Plank, Dee and Julie the design assistants, and the rest of the heroic team. But when the curtains are up, the pictures have been hung and the flowers are in the vase, it is amazing to be part of a fantasy for which so many people have worked so hard – and which ultimately only one person can fully enjoy.

EGYPTIAN

CHAPTER 1

DIN ING ROOM

THE EGYPTIAN BURIAL CHAMBER, carved from rock or shrouded in the heart of a monumental pyramid, is, if you like, the ultimate in getting away from it all. It offers total silence and peace, but also the opportunity to be surrounded by all one's most favourite and precious possessions. The vision of richly coloured wall paintings, golden prizes and mummified pharaohs suddenly revealed in the flickering light of an archaeologist's torch is a highly emotive one.

The sense of discovery is heightened by the inaccessibility of Egyptian tombs, reached through monumental pylon entrances, narrow passages, low-ceilinged spaces and all-encompassing darkness. In ancient Egypt these spaces were linked with the dead of night and the disappearance of Ra, the sun god, into this darkness. The god emerged each dawn to sail his celestial barge across the sky and, in much the same way, the Egyptians believed that the human soul was shrouded in inky blackness until its progression into the bright light of the afterlife.

To help the deceased on their journeys, burial chambers contained maps, instructions and helpful advice conveyed through graphically painted or shallowly carved scenes from the lives of the gods. To make those who had died comfortable,

My original design for Jane's dining room.

anything that had been of use in their mortal existence was buried with them, from the chariot of the warrior to the pen of the scribe. Reminders of everyday life – food, money and even the ancient Egyptian equivalent of Travel Scrabble – tell us how the living lived and how the dead were intended to survive.

The Egyptians appreciated and accepted the inevitability of mortal death and refused to see it as final. On the anniversary of a loved one's departure relatives would gather and feast at the tomb, believing that the deceased was in some way included in their dinner party. At first glance it may seem ghoulish to theme a modern dining room around an Egyptian burial chamber, but the conjunction of the traditions relating to feasting and death with the sepulchral architectural layout of Jane Dunster's dining room gave her fantasy a compelling reality.

EGYPT

From the Renaissance until the eighteenth century Egypt was a mystery to all but a very few Europeans. As part of the Ottoman Empire it was inaccessible, and the only reference material dated from the Romans. If you look at sixteenth- and seventeenth-century depictions of the country you will see an incredible confusion of obelisks and pyramids set in a fantastical landscape. The only ray of reason (as with so many things), was Peter Paul Rubens, who owned Egyptian artefacts, copied them and included them in his paintings.

It was in the eighteenth century that archaeology was

Napoleon's army discovers some Egyptian artefacts on its journey to upper Egypt.

HELENA JAESCHKE
CONSERVATOR

Both Helena and her husband work as conservators at the Petrie Museum in London, and we were lucky enough to be given a private tutorial on its artefacts from ancient Egyptian tombs. Helena told us how the objects were made and described the techniques used and methods of preservation. She also illustrated how tomb paintings were marked out in red ink and then corrected in black. I found it very refreshing to be told by someone with such specialized knowledge that if the ancient Egyptians had had magic markers, they would certainly have used them!

really born, and every now and again you will find a quite spectacularly accurate interpretation of Egypt, such as Piranesi's proposed but never commissioned murals for Florian's in Venice. But the real change began when Napoleon mounted his campaign to conquer Egypt (1798–1801), in which he was defeated and during which Nelson lost his eye. Ever the Citizen Kane character, Napoleon turned a bitter tactical defeat into an aesthetic propaganda triumph.

From the outset, the First Consul had ensured that the camp followers on the campaign should include archaeologists, architects, draughtsmen, surveyors and language experts. At a place called Rosetta one of these stumbled accidentally on the single most important discovery to come from the ancient Egyptian world: a fragment of stone which was to become the Ark of the Covenant, the Holiest of Holies, the seat of all knowledge. For it bore an apparently mundane but, in its consequences, nevertheless world-shatteringly important inscription from the reign of Ptolemy V (205–180 BC), written in Egypt's carefully worked, beautiful – and unintelligible – hieroglyphic symbols but, usefully for language experts, with translations into living Greek and a form of Arabic.

So Napoleon, the great plunderer, returned to France by the skin of his teeth taking with him this key to unlock the secrets of the pharaohs, and all the riches of the Rameses and the Ptolemys for the hungry consumption of the aesthetically sophisticated French Republic. Soon every salon had to include a piece of furniture inspired by the newly fashionable Egyptian style. This quickly travelled to the erudite and cultured court of the Prince Regent in England and inspired architects such as Sir John Soane who, tired of 'Hindoo' and other chinoiserie, incorporated Egyptian motifs into their work.

During the latter part of the nineteenth century, Egypt remained a mysterious, camp and rather vulgar spent force, finding outings only in the stiffest and most academic Salon paintings of the peintres funèbres and Lord Leighton's School. At the century's close the lemming-like hedonism of fin de siècle society revived Cleopatra and the lure of Egypt specifically to shock Victorian mothers.

Egypt's twentieth-century renaissance can be specifically linked to the orange,

A bas-relief of Cleopatra – so characteristic of Egyptian art.

purple, sequin-encrusted explosion that was Diaghilev's Ballet Russe. The opulent slinkiness of the Near East became quite suddenly all the rage on the eve of the First World War. Every demimondaine, every society debutante and, scarily, every toad-like dowager looked in the mirror and imagined herself as Scheherazade, Chloe or, worse, Cleopatra.

Exoticism of this intensity decided quite wisely to keep its head down during the carnage of the First World War. But with the discovery of a perfectly preserved jewel-flooded tomb in 1922, the world drank deeply from the deluge of Egypt fever. Poor, dear Tutankhamun, an unknown, unremarked and unmourned pharaoh, washed once more on to the beach of history and became known for his great taste in turquoise accessories. So Europe went mad again. Mansion blocks sprouted papyrus columns, department stores grew coffered ceilings and star-encrusted vaults and cinemas became temples to Isis and shrines to Hathor.

Since then, the pharaohs have never left our sides. They haunt us from horror films, they cajole us from foam-bath advertisements, they provide us with the steamiest of on-screen kisses and, every now and again, they alter the course of fashion. If Helen of Troy launched a thousand ships, Cleopatra in the guise of Elizabeth Taylor certainly

A colossal statue of Pharoah Rameses II and Queen Nefertari at the temple of Karnak at Luxor.

launched a thousand back-combed bouffants.

It is all too easy to think about the images and personalities of ancient Egypt which are so famous to us today and to run all Egyptian history together into one great exotic chunk. The problem is understanding quite how immense this history really is. More than 5,000 years ago, when our forebears in Brittany, the Iberian peninsula and the British Isles were building primitive tombs and stone circles, Egypt under the pharoah Menes was already notable for its artistic and intellectual achievements, as well as its highly complex hierachy of gods and goddesses.

In this context Cleopatra, who ruled Egypt from 51 to 30 BC, is something of a girl when compared to the generations before her. Picture her, the very embodiment of her country and its heritage in our European eyes, and remember the thousand years or so that had elapsed since Seti I, the great ruler and father of Rameses II, first ordered a chronology of Egypt's rulers to be inscribed in a temple at Abydos near Thebes. He proudly added his name to a list spanning millennia of Egyptian history. Even by his time, the pyramids were more than a thousand years old, as ancient, powerful and mystical to him as they remain to us today.

Egypt was the golden prize of the classical world, the civilization to which all others looked with awe. Its goods were the most highly desired – wheat, gold, the trappings of luxury, indeed civilization itself, were seen to emanate from there. But, in the centuries that followed the death of Cleopatra and the demise of the Egyptian state, the glories of ancient Egypt were all but forgotten and it was Cleopatra who had become the main influence on European culture. She was frequently represented in medieval manuscripts and during the Renaissance she was a potent symbolic character, the embodiment of self-indulgence, opulence and luxurious richness. In Shakespeare's *Antony and Cleopatra* she and Egypt became locked into this personification.

DR DOMINIC MONTSERRAT: EGYPTOLOGIST

Dominic is a senior lecturer in ancient history at Warwick University and author of a number of books. He has spent much time working on archaeological digs in Egypt – but told us that it's not a bit like *Indiana Jones*. His guidelines to the approach we should take to our tomb were very helpful, and he seemed to be generally impressed with the end result although he pronounced it to be 'more temple than tomb'. I think Dominic had a bit of fun with us because we had no idea what the hieroglyphics said until the end. Here is a version of the hieroglyphic alphabet:

Symbol		Pronunciation	Symbol		Pronunciation
	3	'a' as in father		ḫ	'ch' as in loch
	ꞌ	'a' as in car		m	'm' as in moon
	b	'b' as in boot		n	'n' as in normal
	ḥ	'ch' as in Le Havre		p	'p' as in pedestal
	d	'd' as in dog		ḳ	'q' as in queen
	f	'f' as in feel, also 'v' as in viper		r	'r' as in right
	g	'g' as in gopher		s	's' as in saw, also 'z' as in zebra
	h	'h' as in hat		š	'sh' as in show
	ḥ	'h' as in ha		t	't' as in top
	i or ï	'i' as in filled		ṯ	'ch' as in church
	ḏ	'dj' as in adjust		w	'oo' as in too, also 'w' as in wet
	k	'k' as in basket		x	'x' as in x-ray
				y	'y' as in discovery

JANE DUNSTER AND HER VISION

Jane Dunster works as a senior accounts controller for Freeman's catalogue. Although she bought her flat in Penge in south-east London in 1997, she couldn't move in for about a year because it needed a complete renovation before it could be lived in. Jane actually slept in the dining room for several months while the rest of the flat was being decorated, so she already knows what it is like to sleep in her tomb. She loves interior design, and the rooms she has completed herself clearly reflect her innate sense of creativity. In the sitting room she has used wrapping paper (heavily varnished) as a floor covering and in the bedroom crystal drops edge her four-poster bed.

Since early childhood Jane has been passionately interested in the architecture, spiritualism and mysticism of ancient Egypt, sparked initially by her parents' interest in the subject and by watching films like *Death on the Nile*. Busy though she is with her many and varied interests (the gym, collecting Art Deco and Victorian fairies, wine tasting and socializing), she is planning to do a course in Egyptology in the near future. She is also particularly keen on the scarab beetle, both in terms of its industriousness and its symbolic value in ancient Egypt.

Jane knows more about mummification than it is actually healthy to know. The ancient Egyptians believed that the body was the receptacle for the vital life force which survives death, and preserving it so that the person who had died could use it in the afterlife was a crucial part of Egyptian death rites. This meant preserving the internal organs as well as the body itself and the liver, lungs, stomach and intestines were removed and stored in vessels, known to us as canopic jars, protected by the four sons of the sky god Horus. It is interesting that the Egyptians did not consider the brain important enough to be preserved. They believed that the heart was the body's source of all life, and the brain was generally left to rot away in the skull or (hang on to your stomach), stirred into a liquid and left to drain out through the nostrils. Although it later became customary to return the organs to the body after it had been embalmed,

canopic jars were still considered necessary and solid or dummy jars were made. The mummification process was complicated and took up to seventy days to complete. Details of exactly how it was done were never publicly recorded as the process was sacred and undertaken in conditions of secrecy.

How Jane reconciles her deep understanding of such arcane knowledge with day-to-day existence is a complete mystery to me. And how she can comprehend the intricacies of the canopic jar procedure, keep down an extremely successful job and be such a nice person is something that only the Egyptian gods and goddesses themselves can know.

Most people would have shrunk from buying her flat on the grounds that the dining room extension felt tomb-like. Jane bought it *because* it felt tomb-like. And indeed, there was something about the room that spelt ancient Egypt. OK, it had UPVC windows; but they aligned exactly with the passageway entrance. OK, it had a low ceiling; but the centre of gravity pulled one towards Geb, the earth god. As Jane had been brought up on the unique collection of moribund artefacts and wondrousness of ancient archaeology it was not entirely surprising that, with her passion for all things unusual and unexpected, she should be able to tap into this feeling of her dining room space.

Jane's priorities were: number one, tomb; number two, dining room. My problem was to fit the majesty and celestial scale of the Great Pyramid of Giza into the garden extension of a ground-floor flat in Penge.

MY FIRST REACTION TO THE SPACE

There I was, walking down an incredibly narrow passage with a relatively low ceiling. From her kitchen I had had to step down, and into her dining room I would have to step up. The dimensions and proportions of the passageway and the room it led on to made me instinctively want to lie down where her dining table should be with my hands folded across my chest and a lily placed over my heart. It was the first time I had walked into a space and felt as if I was underdressed not wearing a leather jacket, khaki shirt, fedora hat and bullwhip. If, as I had gone in to the dining room, Jane had said, 'Oh mind the boulder, watch the swinging swords and make sure you duck the revolving axe,' I would not have been surprised.

Ahead of me in the room were two UPVC patio doors that opened on to an infinity of metropolitan garden. To my right further UPVC. To my left, two wall lights and nothing else. Behind me lay a bathroom. Beyond me lay a kitchen and in front of me lay a tomb. In the three or four steps I had taken since leaving the comforting bosom of the country-style kitchen, I felt as if I had passed a magical divine journey, tracing the waxing and the waning of the Egyptian sun god. But maybe that was just me.

I could definitely see warm colours working very well. There was a lot of reflected green light from the acres of untended turf in the garden. Never forget that British light is at best green, bouncing off grass, and at worst grey, barging through cloud. There is nothing more welcoming than rich yellow ochre in the British interior. So the paintbox colours of the early tombs were out. I could see it was important we should go for inspiration to the richer earth tones of papyrus scrolls, which conveniently corresponded to

the nineteenth dynasty (c.1342–1200BC) and the reign of Jane's and my favourite pharaoh, Rameses II (he's *the* man).

There was no space for a large diningroom table, and the fact that Jane wanted me to include a sarcophagus as a dining table in the scheme was no help. Praise be to Thoth, protector of scribes and misguided interior designers. For it was he, the ibis-headed great one, who pointed me in the direction of the caravan. For it was in these great people-carriers of the late twentieth century, that I found the divine solution – the flap-down table.

What did tombs have on their floors? I can remember Elizabeth Taylor in Cleopatra flouncing terminally, with an asp persuasively held to her heaving chest, floating across a floor of mirror-black shininess. OK, Jane knew about stirring up brains to make them runny enough to flow through the broken nasal cavity, but she also knew about style. And she knew that the Egyptians had been a synonym for glamour since the earliest times. I was going to give her that floor. I was going to make her room double its size by the prosaic inclusion of a gold vinyl border inset 15 centimetres (six inches) from its perimeter. And I knew that by painting the skirting glossy black, the room would stretch to infinite proportions and Jane could stagger, asp-stung and back-combed like the violet-eyed diva.

But there was still the UPVC. So I decided to ignore the exterior and celebrate the interior by creating an internal facade that spoke of Egypt and all her mysteries and denied the red-bricked Victoriana of south-east London. I decided to build a pylon in front of the windows and to transmute the pesky double-glazed unit on my right into the great solar disc that is propelled by Khepri, the scarab, from its transcendental dawn to its tragic dusk – all out of MDF.

And what of Khepri the scarab, the dung beetle, how was I to re-create him? His shape seems oddly familiar, oddly relevant, oddly lavatory-seat-like.

EXPERTS & HELPERS

ANISSA HELOU: CHEF

A much-travelled, cosmopolitan food writer and author of Middle Eastern Cookery, Anissa prepared our 'dinner with the dead'. It was along the lines of an ancient Egyptian meal:

Baked pigeon stuffed with
   smoked wheat
A traditional Egyptian dish of
   spiced broad beans and pulses
Fresh quarters of raw onion
Garlic sourdough bread
Cucumber
Dates and figs

EGYPTIAN
DINING ROOM
THE PROJECTS

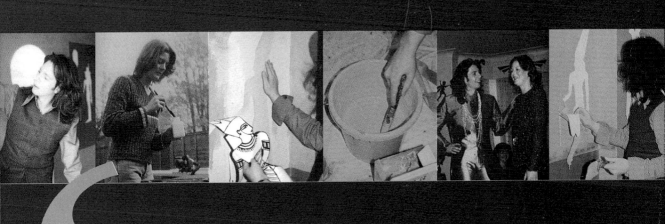

'We should go for inspiration to the richer *earth tones* of *papyrus scrolls.*'

BAS-RELIEFS

No tomb could possibly call itself a tomb without its wall decoration. As was their individualistic and independent bent, the Egyptians created a signature form. Rather than carving in high relief like the Greeks, to give a fully rounded, three-dimensional effect, they sculpted figures and motifs as if they were the top rounded slice of a hard-boiled egg. To which 'bas-reliefs' they added gaudy vegetable-based colours. I decided to give Jane a series of bas-relief deities – without carving into her dampcourse.

- For each of the deities I photocopied a line drawing of an Egyptian god or goddess and blew it up to the right size on a photocopier. I spraymounted the copy to some lining paper and cut it out.

- I spraymounted the image to the wall where it would act as a mask so that the texture I was about to apply to the wall would not affect the area behind the figure.

- I made a paste-like mixture of yellow ochre emulsion, with powder filler (as a thickener) and sand (as a texturizer) and painted this on the wall and over the mask. (I used the same textured paint mixture in the hallway to achieve alternating bands of textured and smooth colour.)

- When the paint was dry I removed the mask from the wall and spraymounted black carbon paper to the back of it. I laid the copy over the shape of the deity and traced the image, line for line, on to the shape and painted the figure with watered-down acrylics in the colours of a papyrus illustration. I used a black marker pen for the hieroglyphics at the base of the figure.

YOU WILL NEED:

Matt emulsion:
  yellow ochre
Sand
All-purpose filler
Spray adhesive
Lining paper
Egyptian
  illustrations
Carbon paper
Artist's acrylic
  colours: yellow
  ochre; red oxide;
  white; Payne's
  grey; emerald
  green; raw
  umber
Black marker pen

EGYPTIAN DINING ROOM

PYLONS

It's one thing to decide that you are going to turn a contemporary dining room into an Egyptian burial chamber, but quite another to incorporate the shapes and materials of modern doorways and windows. Rather than spend time and money changing the actual structure, it is a relatively simple job to create an internal false facade into which the shape of the doorway or window that you want can be cut.

YOU WILL NEED:

Spirit level
String
5 x 2.5cm (2 x 1in)
    timber battens
Screws
18mm (¾in) MDF
Matt emulsion:
    black; dark blue

- I used a spirit level to draw a border around either side of the existing doorway, approximately 30cm (12in) wider than the aperture.

- I deducted 8cm (3in) from each of these uprights and stretched a piece of string from the narrower tops to where the wider border hit the skirting board.

- Our handyman Frank screwed timber battens along the slanted lines of string and cut pieces of 18mm (¾in) MDF to act as the internal and external sides (cheeks) of the pylons. He screwed the MDF to the battens.

- For each pylon, he held a sheet of 18mm (¾in) MDF in place on the face of the cheek, copied the exact outline of the pylon and cut it to shape. He screwed the shape to the cheek to create the ceremonial doorway.

- I used black emulsion as a base coat and dark blue emulsion for the topcoat.

WINDOWS

To disguise the windows I followed the method I had used for the doorway.

- To make the round window that would frame the solar disc I first screwed battens into the wall inside the window frame.

- I used a jigsaw to cut out a circle from a sheet of plywood, just big enough to reveal the amount and shape of window I wanted. I then painted the back of the remaining plywood sheet with black emulsion so that it would not be too visible from the outside.

- I attached the plywood, black side facing outwards, to the battens with screws.

- I used the same method to create slot windows on either side of the door, then made an open box that was the right shape for the pylon out of 18mm (¾in) MDF. I screwed the box straight to the face of the plywood panel I had used to make the slot windows.

YOU WILL NEED:

5 x 2cm (2 x 1in)
   timber battens
Jigsaw
Plywood
Matt emulsion:
   black
Screws
18mm (¾in) MDF

YOU WILL NEED:

Roller blind
Matt emulsion:
    blood red
Acrylic gold size
Gold transfer leaf

SOLAR DISC

I used a lot of gold in this scheme, for the disc, the sarcophagus and elsewhere. It is transfer gold leaf, or Dutch foil, which costs about £5 for a book of twenty-five leaves, rather than the real thing which would have been prohibitively expensive, whereas this is just as effective. Leafing is not a difficult technique to master provided you understand the principles and have the right products.

- I painted a blind red and allowed it to dry, then applied a coat of acrylic size.

- When the size was sticky and completely clear I rubbed the leaf on to the size with my hand and peeled off the backing paper. Given the fact that the leaf is applied to fabric, you have to accept that it will crack, but this just adds to the overall effect.

CANOPIC JARS

As Jane quickly pointed out, every Egyptian tomb should have the mummy's internal organs preserved in alabaster canopic jars. As I quickly pointed out, we were making a dining room. But I took her point and decided to give her a fleet of appropriately hieroglyphed alabaster canopic jars. Relief cream is a paint that comes in a tube and is wonderful stuff. It sets hard and gives a great three-dimensional effect – and also has the added advantage of being extremely easy to apply, just like icing from a piping bag. I used it here, and also for decorative details on the sarcophagus, scarab lavatory seat and furniture – once I had applied the details I used a bronzing kit to bring everything together, following the instructions that came with the kit.

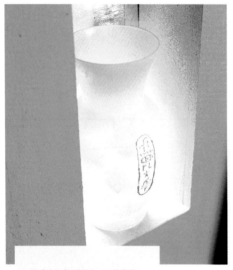

YOU WILL NEED:

Glass vases
Methylated spirits
White enamel
　spray
Cream-coloured
　enamel spray
Topcoat varnish
All-purpose
　interior powder
　filler
Gold relief cream
18mm (¾in) MDF

- I cleaned glass vases with methylated spirits to remove any dirt and sticky deposits, and then sprayed them with white and cream enamel.

- When the enamel had dried I applied a coat of topcoat varnish to each vase and, while this was still wet, sprinkled on some powder filler to give the effect of alabaster. To get an even coverage, I tackled the task in two stages, starting with each vase upside down. When the 'alabaster' was dry I turned the vase the right way up and repeated the process on the remaining surface.

- I applied gold relief cream to create hieroglyphic decorations on the jars.

- To really bring the canopic jars alive, I asked an electrician to change the wall lights into ordinary batten fittings. Frank built a box from MDF to correspond with the size of the jar and fitting, with a hole in the top to allow the light to flood up through the vase and a slot below to both illuminate the wall and allow the bulb to cool.

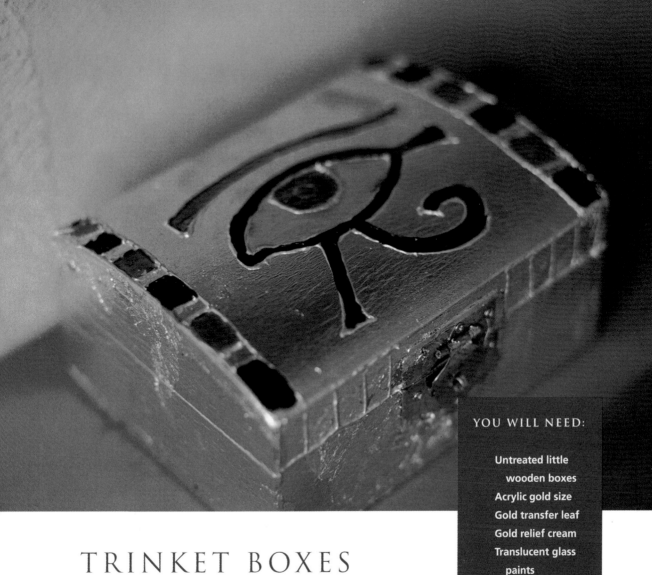

YOU WILL NEED:

**Untreated little
wooden boxes
Acrylic gold size
Gold transfer leaf
Gold relief cream
Translucent glass
paints**

TRINKET BOXES

- The trinket boxes were originally untreated wooden jewellery boxes and the gold leafing was the basis for my fake enamelling technique. Interestingly, this is how enamelling was always done although gold wires were used instead of relief cream, and molten coloured glass was used instead of glass paints.

- I applied gold transfer leaf to the boxes, following the method described for the solar disc.

- Next, I applied relief cream to create wells on the surface of the boxes.

- I painted into the wells using glass paints. The light passes through the translucent paints and bounces off the gold leaf underneath to give a particularly lustrous, enamel-like effect.

SARCOPHAGUS DINING TABLE

The sarcophagus table operates on exactly the same principle as a caravan table and is supported on the decorative table I made.

- Frank cut the sarcophagus out of 18mm (¾in) MDF.

- I attached a concealed tip-latch so that the head of the figure only has to be touched for the table to fall down in a smooth action, and used a piano hinge at the base of the sarcophagus as a pivot.

- I applied gold transfer leaf to the back of the sarcophagus which, when in the down table position, would become the table top, and also gold-leafed the entire area in which the upright sarcophagus would stand.

YOU WILL NEED:

18mm (¾in) MDF
Tip-latch
Piano hinge
Acrylic gold size
Gold transfer leaf
Artist's acrylic
  colours: black;
  grey
Matt acrylic
  varnish
Halogen
  downlight

- I painted my interpretation of a suitably Egyptian figure freehand on the front of the sarcophagus using artist's acrylics in tones of black and grey. I then varnished the figure to preserve it.

- Because the figure is so dark it becomes silhouetted against the gold leaf, so I used a downlight to keep it alive (!) when in the upright position.

DINING CHAIRS AND DAY BED

Seagrass was used to upholster the dining chairs and the day bed for an authentic rush-woven, rustic feel.

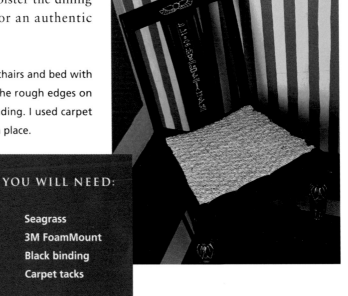

- I stuck the seagrass to the chairs and bed with FoamMount, then bound the rough edges on the day bed with black binding. I used carpet tacks to hold the binding in place.

YOU WILL NEED:

Seagrass
3M FoamMount
Black binding
Carpet tacks

PLEATED CURTAIN

We don't know for sure that the Egyptians had pleated curtains but, as Jane never stopped reminding me, they were big on pleated loin cloths!

- Terry the Pleater pleated a length of white linen and I hung this from a simple curtain pole behind the door pylon with Velcro. I caught the curtain back on one side with a tassel made from jute string.

YOU WILL NEED:

White linen or
    sheeting (which
    you get pleated
    by a specialist)
Curtain pole
Velcro
Jute string

BARREL VAULT

This vault for the hall is my interpretation of a personification of Nut, the sky goddess, who is usually depicted as a woman with her body arched across the stars or even – as here – as a star-spangled sky.

YOU WILL NEED:

18 mm (¾in) MDF
Sheets of 4mm
    (⅛in) plywood
Matt emulsion:
    dark blue
Fairy lights
    without shades
    (100 per string)
Chain
Screw-eye fixing

- I cut 18mm (¾in) MDF formers to fit the exact curve I wanted the finished barrel vault to be and painted 4mm (⅛in) plywood the same dark blue as the pylons.

- I drilled lots of holes into the plywood and pushed the bulbs in a set of ordinary fairy lights through the holes from the back. The wiring was invisible behind the plywood.

- I nailed and glued the plywood to the frame and attached the vault to the ceiling with a chain hanging from a screw-eye fixing, screwed into the ceiling joists.

- An electrician connected the fairy lights to the main light.

THE PRODUCTS

I used the following products in the Egyptian dining room.

BAS-RELIEFS

Dulux matt emulsion: yellow ochre (50YR 31/605)
Sand to mix with paint. DIY stores
Unibond all-purpose filler. DIY stores
3M SprayMount. Stationers; London Graphic Centre
Lining paper. DIY stores
Egyptian illustrations. Ancient Egyptian Designs, The Dover Bookshop
Carbon paper. Stationers
Rowney artist's acrylic colours; white; yellow ochre; red oxide; emerald green; Payne's grey; raw umber
Daler Rowney black marker pen. Stationers; London Graphic Centre

PYLONS

5 x 2.5cm (2 x 1in) timber battens. DIY stores
18mm (¾in) MDF. DIY stores
Dulux matt emulsion: black; dark blue (50BB 08/171)

WINDOWS

5 x 2cm (2 x 1in) timber battens. DIY stores
4mm (⅛in) plywood. DIY stores
Dulux matt emulsion: black; yellow ochre (50YR 31/605)
18mm (¾in) MDF. DIY stores

SOLAR DISC

Roller blind. Homebase
Dulux matt emulsion: blood red (OOYR 08/409)
Acrylic Wundasize. London Graphic Centre
Gold transfer leaf. London Graphic Centre; good art shops

CANOPIC JARS

Glass vases. Homebase
Plasti-Kote White Super Enamel Spray
Plasti-Kote Antique White Super Enamel Spray
Plasti-Kote Fleck Stone Topcoat
All available from DIY stores
Unibond all-purpose interior powder filler. DIY stores
Pebeo Gold Cerne Relief. Good art shops
18mm (¾in) MDF. DIY stores

TRINKET BOXES

Little wooden boxes. IKEA
Acrylic Wundasize. London Graphic Centre
Gold transfer leaf. London Graphic Centre; good art shops
Pebeo Gold Cerne Relief. Good art shops
Pebeo Translucent Glass Paints. Good art shops.

SARCOPHAGUS DINING TABLE

18mm (¾in) MDF. DIY stores
Tip-latch. Homebase
Piano hinge. DIY stores
Acrylic Wundasize. London Graphic Centre
Gold transfer leaf. London Graphic Centre; good art shops
Rowney artist's acrylic colours: black; grey. Daler Rowney
Plasti-Kote Satin Spray Varnish. DIY stores
Halogen downlight. Homebase

DINING CHAIRS AND DAY BED

Seagrass. The Carpet Company.
3M FoamMount. Craft suppliers
Black binding. John Lewis
Carpet tacks. Homebase

PLEATED CURTAIN

White linen or sheeting. Epra Fabrics
Curtain pole. Do It All
Velcro. Haberdashery departments/stores
Jute string. Hardware stores

BARREL VAULT

18mm (¾in) MDF. DIY stores
Sheets of 4mm (⅛in) plywood. DIY stores
Dulux matt emulsion: dark blue (50BB 08/171)
Fairy lights without shades (100 per string). Woolworths
Chain and screw-eye fixing. DIY stores

FLOOR

DMP 78 gold stripping and Pierrot Black VP20. Amtico.
Floor laid by Prestige Flooring.

HALL: WALLS

Unibond all-purpose powder filler and No More Cracks to repair the walls
Easimask masking tape to mark stripes on the walls. Brewers
Lower wall panel: Dulux matt emulsion (90YR 31/605; 53YR 17/504)
Wall motifs. Ancient Egyptian Designs, The Dover Bookshop
Piano hinge to attach shutters. DIY stores
12mm (½in) MDF. DIY stores

MAIN ROOM: WALLS AND CEILING

Dulux matt emulsion (10YY 37/65; 53YR 17/504; 90YR 31/605; 60YR 13/371); dark blue (50BB 08/171)

GENERAL

Moroccan plates and bronze bowls. Talisman Trading
Palm trees. Secret Garden
Garden torches and candles. Price's Patent Candle Company
Art masking fluid. Daler Rowney
Plasti-Kote Gold Leaf Spray. DIY stores
Jali Fretwork Panel, designed to our specifications
Palm leaves and arum lilies. New Covent Garden Market

CHAPTER 2
RITZ

SALON

CÉSAR RITZ, hotelkeeper and former wine waiter, decided to create the most luxurious hotel in London. It was 1906 and any contemporary architect worth his salt was flogging Art Nouveau, sub-Mackintosh straight line-ism or comfy, cosy Queen Anne. César had style. He had served drinks to the most important figures of his day, he had lit the cigarettes of every fashionable lady from Sarah Bernhardt to Alice Keppel. Louis style and only Louis style would do for him. He wanted the grand, processional power of Louis XIV, he wanted the sexual innuendo and oriental indulgence of Louis XV, he wanted the doomed restraint of Louis XVI but, above all, he wanted it gold. He wanted ormolu on top of ormolu, he wanted ormolu on top of damask, he wanted ormolu on top of mirror.

Cesar wanted it all – and he got it. The best and possibly the worst of every Louis style he could lay his hands on. Certainly he knew how to set a scene, knew how to create an atmosphere, knew how to give his paying guests the opportunity to be absolute monarchs for the night and absolute despots in the morning. Michelle Renée has much in common with César. Like him she is drawn to glittery glamour and like him she has a very specific fantasy: she wants the Ritz in her drawing room.

My original design for Michelle's salon.

PICK A LOUIS, ANY LOUIS

*Michelle's heaven -
the Palm Court at
the Ritz.*

The Louis style has always been a candle flame to the grey moths
who are suicidally addicted to glittering ormolu and damask.
Unfortunately for the designers and architects of nineteenth- and
twentieth-century France, it died there in 1793, at the guillotine with the ill-starred Louis
XVI. But elsewhere the power and vortex-like style of the Bourbon kings exerted a
throbbing influence on the cognoscenti of the late eighteenth and nineteenth centuries.
George IV, while Prince Regent, was one of its first collectors, barely five years after the
death of the last Louis.

Louis XIV basically started the style. There had been kings called Louis before him,
but somehow they paled into insignificance compared to the personality and aesthetic drive
of *le roi soleil*. He came to power as a minor in 1643 and during his incredibly long reign,
which lasted until 1715, he retailored the perception of royalty in Europe. He had the best
of his country's aesthetic and political spin doctors to publicize and celebrate his greatness.
Le Brun painted his ceilings. Fouquet sorted out his petty cash and Le Nôtre took the
untidy, messy hand of Mother Nature and turned her into a series of glorious parterres,
tumbling cascades and heavenly gardens. We all know Versailles. And we all know Louis
XIV was a tough act to follow. But Louis XV (his great-grandson) made his mark.

Like Louis XIV, Louis XV assumed the mantle of royalty as a minor. There is the most adorable throne in the seldom-open furniture galleries of the Louvre that was carved for his coronation. It is a confection of gilt, gesso and damson velvet, no less imperial than his predecessor's but built for a boyish monarch. As so often happens, new monarch, new style. Watteau, filmy and delicate recorder of social mores, immortalized the exact moment when the baroque style of Louis XIV gave way to the decorative and domestic French rococo that subsequent generations have universally associated with the entire eighteenth century. The break from the

LOUIS QUELQUE CHOSE

'Louis *quelque chose*' is a term coined by a now unfortunately nameless society decorator. When antiques firmly came into vogue under the famous novelist and interior decorator Edith Wharton, antiquaries and experts shrieked in horror as she mingled furniture and decorative elements from the entire eighteenth century. As far as they were concerned, every Louis had so strong a flavour they could not be tossed together like a random salad.

baroque bastardization of oriental-inspired but classically restrained foliate forms led to the whimsicality and graceful ornamentation of mainstream rococo. Where mirror frames had once been contained by gilded classical columns, now wheelbarrows and stalagmites broke boundaries of architecture and design as befitting the change from the rule of an absolute monarch to that of an absolute mistress: the great style setter and confidante of Louis XV, Madame de Pompadour.

Like any good arbiter of taste, from Cleopatra to Emma Hamilton to the late Princess of Wales, La Pompadour bowed to the winds of change and accepted the Romanized, classicized vision of the future as peddled by the Scottish architect Robert Adam. Thus Louis XVI, the grandson of Louis XV, did not actually have his own style at all. The round-backed chairs and fluted classical legs that go out as Louis XVI should really be known as Louis XV.

To successfully achieve the combination of Louis styles that is the Ritz, we must first

LOUIS 14

unpick a stylistic jumble. To show how the various contrasting elements are combined to such opulent effect, we have to be able to recognize them. As with bouillabaisse, one has to know where cod begins and shellfish ends.

The most efficient way to separate the Louis styles is to try to visualize the clothes that were worn at court. Courtiers at Louis XIV's Versailles were principally vertical. He extended up rather than out; her starched cotton headdress looked like a skyscraper. His richly embroidered veste *à la Turque* reached below the knee and had little exaggerated tailoring to interrupt the vertical line. Her bodice was long

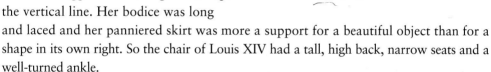

and laced and her panniered skirt was more a support for a beautiful object than for a shape in its own right. So the chair of Louis XIV had a tall, high back, narrow seats and a well-turned ankle.

Madame de Pompadour and her friends revelled in exaggerated contrasts. A small waist became even smaller if hips were padded to infinity; a fresh young face became even fresher if locks were powdered in semblance of senility. So Louis XV chairs grew waists, grew hips, grew wide seats to take upholstered and buckram-stuffed bottoms. The leg of the chair, like the flounce of the skirt, undulated and rippled and asymmetry ruled along with sexual licence.

The chair known as Louis XVI became high waisted and a little more demure. Legs that were once splayed were forced to sit bolt upright. Where monkeys and cranes once played in corners and elbows, pseudo-classical fluting and the ever-present laurel reigned. The typical Louis XV kidney shape became the classically rigid oval or square, but hedonistic decoration continued to abound. Deeply moulded and undercut shells gave way to festoons of equally naturalistic bay leaves. Like thunder on the horizon, change was coming: out with the old, out with the contorted, in with the Republic, off with their heads.

MICHELLE RENEE AND HER VISION

Michelle Renée lives in a one-bedroom, ground-floor rented flat in central London with her husband Beau and her indulged cat Orlando. She is a retired classical dancer and her love of show business is apparent in her photographs of her earlier days, dancing with celebrity chums. After retiring from the stage she ran her own fashion business and now, in her own words, is a lady of leisure. Michelle's home is most definitely her castle. She wants it to be a comfortable and glamorous place to live in but, like so many of us, doesn't have the money to indulge the luxury that is her taste.

She says that her film-director and cameraman father inspired her love of all things glitzy and glamorous, and that she would really like her flat to be like a film set. She loves the energy of London life, the beautiful people and the wonderful buildings. As well as pursuing a beautiful home, her other interests comprise gourmet food, art, ballet and anything to do with Arabic culture.

The completed rooms in her flat already reflect her character and taste. Michelle is very definite in her views and admits to a need to be noticed. Her bathroom has a gold-tented ceiling and fabric on all the walls. Even the loo seat is covered in silk and there are many telephones. Her bedroom is draped in organza and adorned with stars, candles and mirrors.

Michelle is widely travelled and she knows France, she knows Paris and she knows the Ritz on which her fantasy is based. A series of relatively intangible atmospheres gleaned from French architecture, from Versailles to the Hotel Crillon in Paris, also had their effect. In her mind all these influences became one elegant and sophisticated mousse of oyster and champagne, gilt and ormolu, twinkling chandeliers and large mirrored doors. Sitting gazing at her gas fire, she had long cherished the fantasy of large glass doors leading from one wing to another, although the reality of her one-bedroom urban flat belies this magnificence. I could see how seductive the call

of the enfilade was to her. (An enfilade is the French architectural term for the succession of room opening upon room, characteristic of palaces like Versailles. The French have always, quite rightly, hated corridors and have never been obsessed with domestic privacy.)

A word Michelle kept using was 'salon' which, for her, sums up the chattering elegance of female-dominated society in the eighteenth century. Conveniently for such a small flat, it has never been specifically linked to one particular room. In her mind she could see herself reclining underneath a fantastically elaborate canopy while girlfriends and gentleman callers paid court from Louis *quelque chose* spoon-backed chairs. Photographs of her acquaintances and celebrity friends are arrayed around her like a cast of characters in a Molière play, glittering from silver-gilt frames, with star-gazer lilies scenting the air from crystal vases.

The Marie Antoinette Suite at the Ritz – a riot of pastel colours, crystal and gold leaf, the epitome of the Louis style.

EXPERTS & HELPERS

GILES SHEPHERD MANAGING DIRECTOR RITZ HOTEL

Giles is the epitome of a St James's gentleman and has worked at the top end of the London hotel business for thirty years. He was incredibly helpful and allowed us access to some of the Ritz's greatest treasures, which excited Michelle beyond measure. Not only was Giles astoundingly informative about the hotel's history, he added an amusing personal slant as well as a huge battery of anecdotes concerning the daily life of one of London's great institutions.

MY FIRST REACTION TO THE SPACE

Well, the windows were tall, the fireplace almost achieved elegance and the ceilings were high. An interesting architectural anomaly which allowed for a coat cupboard in the hallway had created an enclosed area, almost like a large niche, adjacent to the left-hand window. It made me think of the niche beds incorporated into panelling that were so popular in the aristocratic and intelligent circle which revolved around Madame de Pompadour. Double doors from the living room into the bedroom, though unconventional in the twentieth century were perfectly legitimate for an eighteenth-century apartment; and in the centre of the space, like a vast dusty diadem, was a perfectly serviceable, though rather mass-produced, glass crystal chandelier.

The symmetry and closeness of the windows immediately made me think of the beautiful watercolours I had seen of the original decorations that George IV commissioned for Carlton House, his residence from 1783 when he was Prince of Wales. Rather than having two separate curtain treatments, the old Bourbon junky George decided to create one 'continuous drapery' that linked both apertures. This would work really well in here.

I could see the moss-green carpet replaced most elegantly with a dark timber floor that would reflect the limited light from the overshadowed windows and make the room feel twice the size. Panelling was historically used to keep a room warm. In the late twentieth century its role should be to create an architectural rhythm in a bland and uniform space, and the room certainly had the height for extremely elegant panelling. A pair of false doors mirrored, moulded and gilded on either side of the fireplace would suggest an enfilade, encapsulating the Frenchness and glamour Michelle had always dreamed of. The colour eluded me. I saw colours based on the bloom of a freshwater pearl, atmospheric grey purples that you couldn't actually give a name to. I saw gold, I saw mirror, I saw ivory silk and I saw teasingly pleasing highlights of delphinium. Rather than the preposterously over-gilded furniture of reproduction Louis, I could see chairs painted fresh cream and looking light and giggly against the oyster-coloured walls. I

could also see painted mirror panels, birds on the ceiling, lavender lambrequins and Michelle's ormolu clock mounted on a bracket. Michelle, however, could not envisage this.

Whether you are an interior designer, a shop assistant, or a taxi driver, the client is always right; and it was my job to make Michelle's vision a reality. So as we went along things changed, things were retinted, things were reshaped and things that started off as Louis XV became Louis XXX. But it was Michelle's fantasy and at the end of the project it was she who wept with joy to see it achieved.

FRANCO BARATTA
BUTLER

Franco has been the Ritz's Palm Court butler for thirty-eight years. Since the 1960s he has served tea to the great and good, including royalty and film stars and, as you can imagine, is the soul of absolute discretion. He came to serve us tea in our own salon and agreed that we had achieved the right ambience. This was important because Michelle's fantasy, although based on a few architectural components, was much more to do with intangibles such as smell, light and atmosphere.

RITZ SALON
THE PROJECTS

I could see fresh cream painted chairs looking light and giggly against the oyster coloured walls.

PANELLING

Originally I had felt it would be lovely to give Michelle panels in the style of Louis XV with sophisticated, sexy corners and organic profiles to the tops and sides. These would be easy to achieve by jigsawing a suitably rococo panel shape out of 6mm (¼in) MDF which would be fixed straight to the wall. Michelle's vision, however, was for something much more classical and therefore Louis XVI.

Traditional panelling is based on a straightforward architectural formula which dictates that the wall is divided horizontally into three thirds. The first third constitutes the plinth, more commonly known as the dado. The two remaining thirds become the oblong of the wall itself.

- I cut large 'picture frame' shapes out of 6mm (¼in) MDF that would fill the space between the dado and the cornice, leaving approximately 15cm (6in) grace at both the top and the bottom.

- Two different profiles of commercially available timber moulding were pinned on top of the frames. To make my life easier and to satisfy Michelle's gilt lust, I sprayed them with gold enamel before fixing them securely to the frames.

- The best way to fix 6mm (¼in) MDF to a wall is with high-grab adhesives of the No More Nails school which hold the MDF to the wall permanently. However, they take a while to dry solid so each panel frame was also pinned to the wall at every corner.

- When the frames were on the walls I touched in the pinholes with filler and more gold enamel.

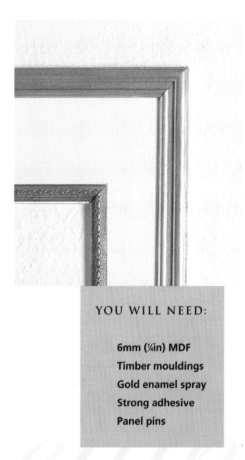

YOU WILL NEED:

6mm (¼in) MDF
Timber mouldings
Gold enamel spray
Strong adhesive
Panel pins

COLOUR

I called the basic colour for the room 'mist monceaux'. Tinting paint to your exact colour is actually quite easy but don't tell any designers I told you so. Paint stains have been used in the decorating industry since time immemorial and are available from good, old-fashioned paint merchants. Always check that a stain operates in the painting medium you will be using – acrylic, oil-based or emulsion – and remember to keep stirring as you apply the tint so that you are not left with clods of colour at the very bottom. Do a test patch on a wall and make your final judgment on the colour when it has dried. I know I always say this, but paint colours when dry look very different to colours in the pot and there is something about the chemistry of paint stains that makes the difference even more pronounced. It is important to retain about one-fifth of the original colour to correct the tint if you find that you have gone too far with the stains.

> YOU WILL NEED:
>
> Matt emulsion:
> magnolia
> Stains: purple;
> orange

- I started with ordinary magnolia emulsion, then added the stains. The colour I had in mind was very subtle, 'transient' as we call it in the trade, and to make sure it did not become too lilac I balanced the purple with orange, which operates as the contrast colour to purple. The combination of the two ensures a more subtle balance of colour.

DAY BED

Both Michelle and Beau are inveterate recliners so it seemed only right to give them a fittingly upholstered and canopied surface to lounge upon. I based this on an ordinary divan bed which I picked up at a junk shop and which, when placed longways against the wall, had the right proportions for a day bed or méridienne.

- I made a simple box cover for the mattress out of ivory silk and attached a box-pleated skirt in a sumptuous gold-striped fabric over the divan base. Two ivory-coloured bolster cushions with gold tassels gave Michelle and Beau somewhere to rest their heads and feet, ivory scatter cushions a support for their backs.

- Above this confection I hung a child's hoop from a chain. This I draped with swagged ivory silk to make an opulent crown, and I hung filmy, crinkle voile to make a sensual veil. A handful of tassels and the whole ensemble denied its origins.

YOU WILL NEED:

Divan
Ivory silk
Striped fabric
Bolster cushions
Scatter cushions
Child's hoop
Chain
Gold tassels
Crinkle voile

TABLE AMBULANTE

Because rooms were only given specific names and functions in the twentieth century, Louis interiors relied upon a series of small portable pieces of furniture that allowed people to eat in whichever room they felt was appropriate to their mood or outfit. Tables ambulantes, literally 'walking tables', were moved from a corner of the room and placed adjacent to whichever chair, couch or méridienne the master or mistress wished their meal to be served at. This suited Michelle to a T.

- I obtained a pretty, MDF table with elegant Louis XV legs (I always think these legs with their vestigial knees really look as if they could walk around the room), and very simply painted it with magnolia emulsion.

- To make the emulsion durable, I applied several coats of tinted antiquing wax, rubbing each layer into the grain of the MDF to achieve a water-resistant finish. In my experience this is a more efficient way of duplicating old worn paint than using antiquing glazes.

YOU WILL NEED:

**Elegant table
made from MDF
or untreated
timber
Matt emulsion:
magnolia
Antiquing wax**

YOU WILL NEED:

18mm (¾in) MDF
Gold leaf enamel
spray
Strong adhesive
Plastic mouldings

PELMET

The pelmet goes over both windows and to create interest I brought its line forward on both sides in front of the central plaque. The centrepiece of the pelmet is made from real plaster and the mouldings on either side are plastic.

- The main panels, side panels and two dome-topped shapes (known as aedicules) were cut from 18mm (¾in) MDF and I sprayed them with gold leaf enamel.

- I glued the plaster centrepiece and plastic mouldings on to the pelmet. At either end I used the dome-topped pieces of MDF, which would relate to the vertical drape of ivory silk that I planned to attach below them.

EXPERTS & HELPERS

MARK MORALEE
DECORATIVE
PLASTERER

The London Cornice Company is a young company specializing in recasting intricately moulded cornices and plaster architectural embellishments for Georgian, Edwardian and Victorian homes. Their incredibly high standard of workmanship and attention to detail made them a perfect choice for work at Buckingham Palace. Mark found a lovely carved wooden overdoor which he cast in plaster for me so that I could use it as the central plaque in Michelle's pelmet.

MIRRORED DOORS

The driving force behind Michelle's fantasy seemed to be the creation of fictional rooms beyond her small flat. Putting large expanses of mirror in a room does an enormous amount for increasing its size and lightness.

- To give Michelle that grand, mirrored-door feel, I asked Frank to screw frames made of 5 x 2.5cm (2 x 1in) timber battens to either side of the fireplace.

- Frank attached an 18mm (¾in) sheet of MDF to each frame and screwed heavy French-style timber mouldings around the perimeters. He glued sheets of mirror, which had been cut to size, inside the frames then cut two tall, thin slots in pieces of 6mm (¼in) MDF and fixed these on top of the mirrors.

- To get the right panel shapes Frank gilded lengths of moulding with gold leaf enamel spray and attached them horizontally across the mirrors. Being a crafty carpenter, he also provided me with a vertical rout in the MDF between the two 'doors', which impressed me enormously.

- Anything not already gold was then painted in magnolia gloss.

- We attached heavy brass handles and at once I really felt that there were two large doors either side of the fireplace.

- Since Michelle had two rather pretty plaster plaques knocking around, we decided to incorporate them as overdoors, screwing them to the wall and adding a mitred moulding to the top. The central bow of each was then loose-leaf gilded (see page 51).

YOU WILL NEED:

6mm (¼in)
Timber battens
18mm (¾in) MDF
Decorative
timber
mouldings
Mirrors cut to size
Screws
Strong adhesive
Gold leaf enamel
spray
Gloss paint:
magnolia
Polished brass
handles
Acrylic gold size
Loose-leaf gold

CURTAIN TREATMENT

All the Louis loved beautifully and intricately embroidered fabrics to wear, to sleep in, to kiss in and to drape their windows with. The closest we can get to these fantastically extravagant pieces of figured silk are the beautifully embroidered saris that are normally reserved for Asian brides. These can cost anything up to £1,000 – or more. I managed to buy an exquisite ivory silk sari with an ornate gold border for under £150. This is more than enough fabric – about 4 metres – to create an opulent pelmet for two windows, provided the cloth is cut wisely.

- Every sari has one end which is much more embroidered than the other and before I started to make the curtains I cut this off the one I had bought.

- I cut the remaining fabric in two lengthways to create two panels and staple-gunned these to the inside of the MDF pelmet, allowing the soft silk and heavy gold borders to drape across the windows.

- I then cut the richly embroidered end piece vertically to create two tails which I staple-gunned on either side of the space between the windows (known historically as the 'pier').

- Beneath the aedicules I used two lengths of ivory silk and caught each one up with a heavy gold tassel approximately two-thirds from the floor. I then pulled each length of fabric through its tassel to create a 'balloon'.

- To filter the light in as flattering a way as possible, I hung crinkle voile sheers which I had edged with a cheap bobble fringe sprayed with gold leaf enamel. The whole effect was completed by a pair of brass hold-backs rather romantically known by the French as embraces or 'kisses'.

- Finally, I installed two simple white roller blinds to stop people looking in at night.

EXPERTS & HELPERS

PINKY
SARI SELLER

Pinky works in Cuckoo Fashions, one of many sari shops in Whitechapel in the East End of London. She keeps a huge range of colours and designs and I often use the shop as a supplier. Pinky is always a riotous fund of East End gags and colourful stories. She picked out the gorgeous sari we used for the curtain treatment from a special glass cabinet, where she keeps her most precious saris, specifically designed for weddings and celebrations. I am completely addicted to saris and Pinky always goes out of her way to find the exact colour combination or pattern I need, as well as entering into the spirit of the design scheme.

YOU WILL NEED:

Sari
Staple gun
Ivory silk
Gold tassels
Crinkle voile
Bobble fringe
Gold leaf enamel
     spray
Brass hold-backs
Roller blinds

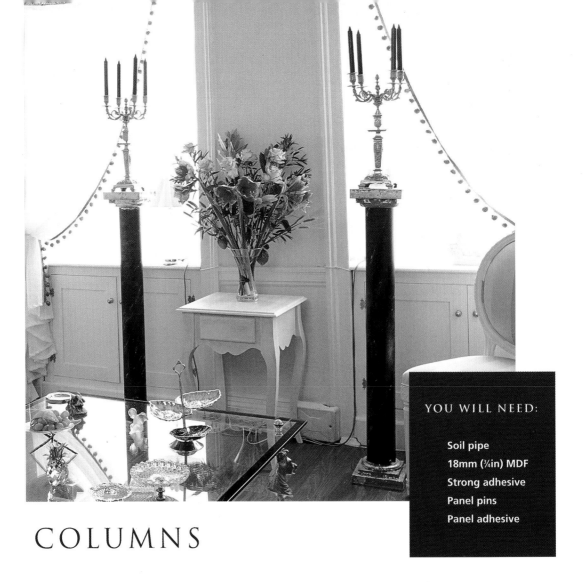

YOU WILL NEED:

Soil pipe
18mm (¾in) MDF
Strong adhesive
Panel pins
Panel adhesive

COLUMNS

Poo pipe (all right, it's really known as soil pipe) can be bought from most DIY merchants and is of a suitable girth to inspire comparisons with plinth-height columns.

- Frank cut two lengths of pipe at 1.2m (4ft) and then, for each pipe, he cut two discs of 18mm (¾in) MDF which he checked would fit snugly into the top and bottom of the pipe.

- For each pipe he cut two discs, both approximately 2.5cm (1in) greater in diameter than the pipe and four pieces of MDF that were the square of the discs, that is, the discs fitted exactly into the squares.

Two of the squares were slightly larger than the others. For each end of the pipe he glued and pinned a smaller disc, a larger disc, a smaller square and a larger square together. He then popped one of these combinations in the top and one in the bottom of each pipe. The smaller discs fitted like the lids in a tube of sweets. The fit may be so tight that no further fixing is needed, but a good splodge of panel adhesive will make sure that they stay firmly in place.

MARBLING THE COLUMNS

I had a fascinating time learning how marble paint effects are achieved by a true professional, Keith Warwick.

- Keith made up his own acrylic satinwood base by mixing black emulsion and satin acrylic varnish and painted this on to the soil pipe. When you are marbling, you need a base coat that is shiny and slippery enough to allow you to move the paint around to achieve the right effect.

- When the base coat was dry he mixed some pale grey acrylic paint into acrylic scumble glaze. Scumble glaze is specifically designed to slow down the drying time of paint, allowing you to rag, drag, flog or flag to your heart's content. In this case Keith sponged the grey on with a natural sponge to create a blotchy starting point for the marble technique. Before it dried he softened it with a dry brush.

- For the veining Keith used a brush with extremely long hairs. He mixed a very pale grey acrylic (almost white), and then a red oxide colour. He then dipped the brush in both colours allowing one side to be grey and the other side to be red – this sounds tricky, but how often does this happen when you don't need it?

- He set to work painting in the veins. To do this, he used the point of the brush to create a thin line and then allowed the flat of the brush to drag more paint across the surface to thicken the line up as he went along. By alternating these techniques, he achieved a

> **YOU WILL NEED:**
>
> **Matt emulsion:**
> **black**
> **Satin acrylic**
> **varnish**
> **Brushes, including**
> **a long-haired**
> **brush**
> **Artist's acrylic**
> **colours:**
> **white; black;**
> **Payne's grey;**
> **red oxide**
> **Acrylic scumble**
> **glaze**

very convincing thick-thin veining that is characteristic of most marbles.

- As a finishing touch he softened each vein with a dry brush, working in the opposite direction to that in which the vein was travelling. For a real cheat, I have often used the impression of a piece of cling film on top of wet scumble glaze which can, at a distance (and don't tell Keith), pass for marble if you squint your eyes and have never seen a piece of real marble. With this method, the finishing touch is several coats of glossy varnish.

GILDING THE COLUMN BASES

Gold leaf comes in two flavours – transfer leaf ('Dutch foil') or loose leaf. The rest of us are more than content with the Dutch variety. This transfer leaf is backed by paper that resembles greaseproof paper and is easier to work with. The principle is the same for both. A sticky glue, or size, is applied to the area that you want gilded and the leaf is applied and burnished so that joins and seams disappear. These days we are lucky to have acrylic

YOU WILL NEED:

Acrylic gold size
Gold transfer leaf

gold size which is workable within ten minutes or so, unlike oil size which has to be left for twenty-four hours before the leaf can be applied. Acrylic gold size is the colour of milk when it is first applied, and goes completely clear when it is sticky enough.

Artificial gold leaf, or Dutch metal, is not expensive – about £5 for a book of twenty-five leaves. Real gold leaf or loose leaf (22.5 carats) costs about £1 a leaf. Real devotees, Michelle included, can spot the difference.

- If you are using gold transfer leaf, start by applying acrylic gold size with a brush to the base of the column. Elena Vinycomb, our master gilder, gave me an excellent tip, which is to tint the size so that you know exactly where you have painted, allowing you to fill in any missed bits before the size is ready.

- Gently rub the leaf on to the size with your fingers and peel off the paper. This should come away easily, just like a transfer.

- Use a clean, soft cloth to burnish the leaf.

- Like all things, practice makes perfect, so it would be a good idea to try the technique out on something simple first to get a feel for how to work with the leaf.

EXPERTS & HELPERS

KEITH WARWICK
MARBLER

Keith is one of a long line of specialist paint technicians that stretches as far back as the Romans. It is inconceivable to us today, but it was more cost-efficient to employ the great Giotto to paint fake marble than it was to use the real thing. Marbling is a relatively complicated technique but Keith, as well as knowing all the short cuts and tricks of the trade, could get the basic points across without using jargon. He is also one of the few specialists in this field who has embraced technological advances in the paint industry. The best thing about him, however, was that he was completely unfazed when faced with a couple of soil pipes and told that I wanted them to look like marble columns.

ELENA VINYCOMB: GILDER

Elena is one of a new generation of young people committed to practising traditional crafts and was a real find – she had in fact been commissioned by the Ritz to regild large areas of its ground floor a few years ago, so Michelle's room received gilding of the highest and most traditional standards. Immensely knowledgeable and very experienced, Elena showed us the techniques for, and differences between, loose-leaf and transfer-leaf gilding. Elena also specializes in murals and decorative paint techniques, some of which had not seen the light of day in 200 years.

LOOSE-LEAF GILDING

The following is a précis of our expert's work. Anyone wanting to use loose-leaf gold will need highly specialized equipment, including a suede pad with a 'tent' made of parchment. Since you cannot touch loose leaf – it will stick to anything sticky or oily, even the cleanest fingers – you need something to stop the leaf blowing away.

• Through an incredibly complicated, rather nerve-racking procedure similar to the extraordinary dough-chucking antics of an experienced pizza chef, Elena managed to get a piece of loose leaf from the book it came in on to the suede pad using the broad blade of a gilder's knife.

• She used the sharp edge of the knife to cut the leaf into appropriate squares and then did something very strange: she took a dry brush and brushed it on her cheek, apparently to collect enough grease to pick up the gold.

• With the leaf attached to the brush with nothing but her own sebum, she transferred the leaf from the pad to the area that had been sized.

MIRROR FRAME

Michelle fell in love with the hugely ornate mirror frames in London's Wallace Collection, so I thought I would do my best to come up with something that had all the opulence and grandeur of a Louis-style museum-piece.

- I cut a piece of 6mm (¼in) MDF in the approximate asymmetrical profile of a Louis XV mirror frame.

- I then used plastic rococo mouldings to edge the frame with a series of volutes and curlicues. I attached these with a hot glue gun and, using the same adhesive, stuck real dried bay leaves at the top and bottom of the frame.

- For more delicate detail I used gold relief cream in a lattice pattern down either side of the frame.

- I sprayed the frame with a spray primer and, when this was dry, believe it or not I sprayed it with water from a plant sprayer. Bear with me on this one. Before the water dried I then sprayed gold leaf enamel over the entire frame. The droplets of water caused the enamel to bubble in a very subtle, light-catching way that made the frame look a little classier than a lump of MDF, a handful of plastic and a strewing of vegetation.

- Finally, I gave the frame several liberal coats of permanent spray adhesive and quite randomly applied gold transfer leaf all over it.

YOU WILL NEED:

MDF or untreated
timber
Suitably shaped
firescreen
White primer
Matt emulsion:
magnolia
Translucent glass
paints
Brass embossing
foil
Strong adhesive
Hot glue gun

FIRESCREEN

I wanted one item to bring everything together and decided that a little firescreen to distract the eye from Michelle's rather un-Louis gas fire would be the best thing.

- I started with an MDF firescreen with a suitably Louis profile and applied several broken coats of white primer and magnolia emulsion to create a cloudy effect.

- When the paint was dry I drew a decorative motif and a garland of big, fat Aubusson roses which I painted with glass paints to create the translucent colours of eighteenth-century china. A good tip when painting pink roses like these is always to use an orangey scarlet in dark areas, such as inside the flower itself. This helps to create the

delicate transparency the great china painters at Sèvres and Meisen achieved with their coloured china glazes.

- For a finishing touch I used brass embossing foil which I cut into the approximate shape of a Louis ormolu mount.

- To achieve the appropriate detailing on the surface of the foil I used an ordinary ballpoint pen on the reverse of the foil: the lines come through as ridges. Finally I used a hot glue gun to attach the foil to the firescreen.

CAT BED

As a little present for Michelle and her familiar Orlando, the talking cat, I asked Frank to make a perfect scaled-down Louis XV fauteuil or upholstered armchair.

- Frank made a simple shovel shape from 18mm (¾in) MDF and cut an appropriately swirling rococo profile into the top and sides. I painted it with magnolia emulsion.

- I gilded off-the-shelf miniature Queen Anne legs and Frank fixed them to the shovel shape with screws.

- All we then needed was a luxurious, plump tassled cushion and a spoiled cat in a jewelled collar.

Cat Bed

YOU WILL NEED:

18mm (¾in) MDF
Matt emulsion:
    magnolia
Queen Anne legs
Acrylic gold size
Gold transfer leaf
Screws
Tasseled cushion

THE PRODUCTS

I used the following products to create the Ritz salon.

PANELLING
6mm (¼in) MDF.
    DIY stores
Timber mouldings.
    Winther Browne
Plasti-Kote Antique Gold
    Enamel Spray. DIY stores
No More Nails adhesive.
    DIY stores
Panel pins. DIY stores

COLOUR
Johnstone's Cova Plus
    matt emulsion:
    magnolia (CemaG5)
Universal Stainers stains:
    purple; orange. Leyland
    Paints

DAY BED
Divan. Junk shop
Ivory silk. Broadwick Silks
Nina Campbell striped
    fabric. Osborne & Little
Bolster cushions.
    John Lewis
Scatter cushions.
    John Lewis
Child's hoop. Good toy
    shops
Chain. DIY stores
Gold tassels. Stylogue
Crinkle voile. Stylogue

TABLE AMBULANTE
GT1/W Gustavian writing
    desk. Scumble Goosie
Johnstone's Cova Plus
    matt emulsion:
    magnolia (CemaG5)
Antiquing wax. Liberon

PELMET
18mm (¾in) MDF. DIY
    stores
Plasti-Kote Gold Leaf
    Enamel Spray.
    DIY stores
No More Nails adhesive.
    DIY stores
Plastic mouldings.
    Shortwood Carvings

MIRRORED DOORS
5 x 2.5cm (2 x 1in) timber
    battens. DIY stores
6mm (¼in) and 18mm
    (¾in) MDF. DIY stores
HC33 timber mouldings.
    Winther Browne
Mirrors cut to size. Glass
    Express
No More Nails adhesive.
    DIY stores
Plasti-Kote Gold Leaf
    Enamel Spray. DIY stores
Johnstone's Cova Plus
    gloss: magnolia
    (Cema G5)
Polished brass 'Acquitaine'
    handles. Clayton Munroe
Acrylic Wundasize.
    London Graphic Centre
Gold loose leaf.Cornelissen

CURTAIN
TREATMENT
Sari. Cuckoo Fashion
Ivory silk. Broadwick Silks
Gold tassels. Stylogue
Crinkle voile. Stylogue
Bobble fringe. John Lewis
Plasti-Kote Gold Leaf
    Enamel Spray.
    DIY stores
Brass hold-backs.
    Do It All
White roller blinds.
    Homebase

COLUMNS
Soil pipe. Builder's
    merchants
18mm (¾in) MDF.
    DIY stores
No More Nails adhesive.
    DIY stores
Panel pins. DIY stores

MARBLING THE
COLUMNS
Dulux matt emulsion:
    black
Dulux satin acrylic varnish
Artist's acrylic colours:
    white; black; Payne's
    grey; red oxide. London
    Graphic Centre
Polyvine acrylic
    scumble glaze

GILDING THE
COLUMN BASES
Polyvine acrylic
    gold size.
Gold transfer leaf. London
    Graphic Centre

MIRROR FRAME
6mm (¼in) MDF. DIY
    stores
Plastic mouldings.
    Shortwood Carvings
No More Nails adhesive.
    DIY stores
Hot glue gun. DIY stores
Pebeo Gold Cerne Relief.
    Good art shops
Plasti-Kote spray primer.
    DIY stores
Plant sprayer. Do It All
Plasti-Kote Gold Leaf
    Enamel Spray.
    DIY stores
3M PhotoMount spray
    adhesive. Office suppliers
Gold transfer leaf. London
    Graphic Centre

FIRESCREEN
FS5 Queen Anne
    firescreen.
    Scumble Goosie
White primer. DIY stores
Johnstone's Cova Plus
    matt emulsion
magnolia (Cema G5)
Pebeo Translucent Glass
    Paints. Good art shops
Brass embossing foil.

Hobby/model shops;
    Homecrafts Direct
No More Nails adhesive.
    DIY stores
Hot glue gun. DIY stores

CAT BED
18mm (¾in) MDF. DIY
    stores
Johnstone's Cova Plus
    matt emulsion:
    magnolia (CemaG5)
Queen Anne legs. Relics of
    Whitney
Polyvine acrylic gold size.
Gold transfer leaf.
    London Graphic Centre
Tasseled cushion. Stylogue

FLOOR
Wood-effect Rhodesian
    mahogany. Do It All

GENERAL
CC220 carver. Wychwood
    Design
DC220 dining chair.
    Wychwood Design
Ivory damask lampshades.
    British Home Stores
Noritake white palace
    bone china and silver
    teapot/tray. China
    Presentations
Glass panelled doors.
    Wickes
Flowers. Rosalie Owen
Corbels. Winther Browne
Plaster corbel and plaque.
    The London Cornice
    Company
Pink Limoge drop handles.
    Clayton Munroe

CHAPTER 3
ROMAN LIVING ROOM

THERE IS SOMETHING ABOUT THE ROMANS that continues to speak directly to the British and, although the Saxons and Angles, and ultimately the Normans, overran us after the fall of the empire, we look back at Rome as our favourite conqueror. Of course, until recently we would have had a major interest in common with the Romans: we could have chatted at length with them about the responsibilities of running an empire, swapped jokes about what it is like to be one of the world's most powerful nations and generally bonded with a fellow imperial bully. So while the Shadrakes' fantasy room – a fifth century AD Roman interior in a modern town house in Essex – may seem incongruous at first glance it has a pretty forceful relevance, not as only as part of the national psyche but also geographically: the Romans adored Essex, they loved Colchester and greedily annexed Chelmsford as a Roman suburb.

THE ROMAN IN BRITONS

Roman design, Roman architecture and Roman decoration are among the most important influences on western culture. Although other civilizations have had their effect, the classical world has been the benchmark for aesthetic judgement since the Renaissance. In Britain, in particular, an affinity with Rome has survived the centuries.

I think the overriding attraction the Romans hold for us is their absolute dedication to the straight line. We love their down-to-earth practicality, which led them to become the best organized of the ancient civilizations – music to British ears. Aesthetically speaking, what really turns us on about them is their obsession with engineering over form. The Greeks created beautiful art, the Romans built fantastic foundations. Their complete commitment to the internal workings of any architectural structure or mechanical device is comparable to our own. Every great building in Britain cloaks itself in a style developed by one of our foreign competitors, but the actual methods of construction, the nuts and bolts nitty-gritty, are all our own. The architects of the seventeenth and eighteenth centuries created aesthetically pleasing buildings for their great and courtly patrons, but the untrammelled pride in engineering fanned by the Victorian flame had huge ramifications on the development of architecture in the twentieth century. Think of the monuments that celebrate the end of the millennium. None are conceived as buildings. All are cathedrals to the cleverness of clever engineers, with tensioned hausers, sleek polypropylene and external service ducts. It is as if we have always found the aqueduct sexier than the aedicule.

As the colonizers of a chilly island the Romans were quick to deploy their already burgeoning skills as central heating engineers. They also allowed themselves free reign as town planners and builders of straight roads. Although pre-Roman Britain was in no way savage, the large-scale organization imposed by the Romans was unheard of

DR PAUL SEALEY
ARCHAEOLOGIST

Paul is assistant curator at Colchester Castle and something of a fanatic when it comes to life in Roman Britain. He told us about the history of the castle and showed us the vaults of the Temple of Claudius on which it was built. He also described, in vivid and graphic detail, how Boudicca sacked the temple. Paul gave us his verdict when we had completed the project and we were proud to have achieved an authentic interior.

My original design for the Shradrakes' living room.

Roman mosaics achieved all the sophistication of Greek paintings on which they were based. (Roman pavement mosaic, AD 1-2.)

in the scattered, competitively tribal societies that peppered the countryside. Therefore the impact of something as simple as a paved, straight road cannot be overestimated.

To begin with the Britons resisted annexation by the mighty empire and the island known as Britannia was one of its least peaceable and least Romanized provinces. It took two military expeditions by Julius Caesar to defeat them, in 55 BC and a year later in 54 BC when five Roman legions and 2,000 horsemen faced the war chariots of Cassivellaunus, a powerful enemy who was the chieftain of a tribe in what are now Hertfordshire, Buckinghamshire and Berkshire. Nearly 120 years later Boudicca, the widow of Prasutagus, king of Iceni (Norfolk), led a revolt against the Romans and sacked Colchester, London and St Albans. But Britannia had a strong agricultural economy and was rich in mineral resources. The Romans persevered and by AD 85 they controlled all of Britain south of the Clyde river.

The first major drive towards colonization started around the Thames basin, where the most densely populated towns were situated. Londinium (London) was already an active river port and became the centre of the Roman road system. A busy eastern route led to the important colony of Camulodunum (Colchester), and continued on to Lindum (Lincoln) and Eburacum (York). Another important road went west, through Silchester to the land of the Silures (in what is now Wales).

Testimony to the might, ingenuity and determination of the Romans can be found throughout the British Isles. It is hard, for example, to remember that Hadrian's Wall was built virtually 2,000 years ago in AD 122. Stretching from the Solway Firth to the mouth of the Tyne, it is 115 kilometres (72 miles) long and was constructed to defend Britannia's northern borders against Caledonian invaders.

Everywhere the Romans colonized, they left examples of the high level of civilization and culture they enjoyed in all aspects of their lives. Sophisticated buildings

FANTASY ROOMS

designed for living the Roman way remain, at least in part, in most major areas of occupation in Britain. The pickings are particularly rich in cities along old supply routes and we know how the Romans lived from what they left for us to dig up hundreds of years later. We know, for example, about their predilection for bathing – the well-preserved Roman baths in the city of Bath illustrate the religious significance of natural springs and how this translated itself into everyday life. Not only physical comfort, but theatre, art, architecture, music, food and entertaining, communication, travel, military strength and manufacturing were as essential to Roman society as they are to today's great civilizations.

In the fifth century the Britons were truly Romano-British. They revelled in their organized society, its smooth-running infrastructure and the seductive pleasures of plumbing. But by now the empire was hugely overextended. The once blisteringly efficient supply lines were stretched taut and eventually, when Rome was challenged by the Germanic tribes, they snapped. To staunch the flow of power from the violently opened imperial arteries, the Roman legions were recalled from Britain to protect the moribund heart of the once great civilization, and the rich plunder of Britain fell prey to the wolfish pagan Saxons and Angles.

Hadrian's Wall. The impact of Roman engineering
on the British countryside is still with us today.

THE SHADRAKES
AND THEIR VISION

Dan and Sue Shadrake live in a 1960s semi-detached house in Basildon, Essex. Dan is a graphics supervisor and Sue has recently retired after twenty-five years in the civil service. They are, individually and together, passionate about the Romans.

Dan was born with the Roman bug. He saw Roman armour in Colchester Castle when he was a boy and became hooked. While most of his friends played outside he locked himself in his room with his books, poring over historical novels about Roman Britain and, of course, Asterix the Gaul – who has to be ancient Rome's foremost sales representative in recent times. His film greats are *Ben Hur* and *Julius Caesar*. Dan is the founder of The Britannia Society, the only group in Britain that re-enacts late-Roman battles. Its members first met in his sitting room and there are now fifty of them. Dan says he is not a trainspotter about Roman things, he is just 1,500 years out of date.

Originally fascinated by the Normans, Sue was eventually seduced by the persuasive charms of The Britannia Society. Her family are from the Essex area and she feels she might be descended from the Romans. She felt drawn to the past long before she met Dan, a meeting which seems to have been fated: she was trekking with her dogs for a month, trying to discover what was missing from her life, when she came across a poster for the Britannia Society – which led her to Dan, marriage and a fantasy to be shared.

Of all the people I met on the television series, Dan and Sue were the only couple to live out their fantasy with such relish. They are prepared to spend all evening enjoying an impassioned but tender debate on the exact configuration of a legionary's chinstrap. And I very much got the feeling that they would have been more than happy if they did not have to rejoin the twentieth century on Monday morning after a weekend immersed in Roman Britain. Their fantasy has such a detailed personality that it has almost become an alter ego.

It is this closely researched interest in every aspect of Roman life that ensures that the Shadrakes bring an engaging element of reality to their fantasy. Although they have an irresistible urge to turn time back and live in the fifth century, they see themselves as ordinary Roman Britons. Most period fantasists are drawn to the top end of the historical market. Who ever admits to wanting to be a filthy, pox-ridden beggar, stepped over by the bewigged bourgeoisie of the day? Dan and Sue see themselves transported back in time but living the kind of life they live now – and their refreshing commitment to each other means there is nothing they would change if they were given a completely different, albeit retrospective, lifetime.

There is something rather clean and wholesome about falling in love with the Romans. Their branding is nearly always positive, as team players, as gentlemen, as one of us. Except, of course, for the wildly excessive, decadent and debauched courts of the emperors. Resplendent with towering columns, gilded busts, imported mosaics and imported slaves, the palaces of Caligula or Nero tinkled with theatrical glamour. My vision of a Roman living room, I have to say, would be for the cruelly monumental – debauchery and all.

Sue and Dan wanted a rustic outpost of the empire – a common or garden room for a frontiersman, rather than a palatial sala built for an emperor or ex-pat pharaoh. Villa Shadrake had to be rugged (and I don't mean strewn with rugs). It had to have homespun elements and an overriding cosy sense of home. Cosy, that is, in a Roman way. Although the Shadrakes' commitment to the period and specialist knowledge of the era set the tone for many of the decorative solutions, comfort and practicality had to govern the scheme. The Romans knew practicality backwards – the challenge was to provide the Shadrakes with the level of comfort offered by their inappropriately contemporary green leather sofa.

ASTERIX

There is a generation that has been almost entirely weaned on the highly descriptive vision of local ancient history drawn by Goscinny and Uderzo. In their Asterix books they created a Romanized world in which every other speech bubble contained a playground pun. In *Asterix in Britain*, all the amusing foibles of late-twentieth-century suburban life are reflected in Britain in 54 BC. Houses have names, not numbers, and are laid out in infinite, ordered, metroland grids – completely contrary to archaeological evidence, but entirely complementary with our national view.

MY FIRST REACTION TO THE SPACE

The Shadrakes' predilection for both Roman life and practicality had guided them to install a quarry tile floor and I knew this would work. My old adversary, UPVC windows, could be made invisible behind Roman-like fretwork shutters, and the newly plastered walls would prove the perfect surface for the bordered and panelled painted wall treatments of the late Roman period.

The Shadrakes had divided the long narrow room with a brick wall which sprang at right angles to the fireplace. This gave us the opportunity to create separate atmospheres in two spaces. The garden room felt smaller but brighter and could therefore become an 'atrium'. This usually formed the centre of a Roman house and acted as a light-well and water butt. Rain water was siphoned into a hole in the roof and through elaborately cast funnels that we would today call 'gargoyles', into a shallow pool below. A fountain often circulated the water and a concealed cistern below the pool always stored water for household use. Removing a section from the ceiling was never a real option, but creating the feeling of light with a highly reflective surface would prove a viable piece of visual trickery. The inner part of the room could be used as a dining area.

Sue and I were greatly inspired by our visit to the Museum of London, the most important inspiration for the scheme being Roman wall paintings. Richly coloured panels framing brightly coloured vignettes or decorative figures have inspired generations of designers over the centuries. Raphael was lucky enough to be present at the unearthing of the Baths of Trajan, and the elegant wall paintings he saw at first hand inspired

not only him and his school but also the rest of the western world.

The vast expanse of unfurnished hall at the Shadrakes' house gave me a fantastic opportunity to indulge my love for Roman wall painting. I took great pleasure in preparing a series of architectural and figurative motifs to embelish the Shadrakes' wall panels. In the end, however, on surveying the finished effect, both Paul Sealey and I agreed that my frescoes were more neo-classical than purely classical.

ROMAN
LIVING ROOM
THE PROJECTS

'Villa Shadrake *had to be*

rugged (and I don't mean

strewn with rugs).'

FANTASY ROOMS

ROMAN WALL PANELS

Using strongly contrasting paint colours in an architectural way does a lot to increase the feeling of space in a room. I'm not sure that the Romans had this in mind when they painted decorative panels on the walls of their town houses and villas, but the definite relationship between the reds and blacks they used with, every now and again, a paler cream, created a tremendous sense of rhythm and spaciousness. They often divided the height of a room in three, taking the bottom third as the plinth, and then splitting each wall vertically by the proportion of the plinth. As ever with the Romans, creativity came second to carefully worked out structure.

- I drew plans of the walls to a 1:10 scale on graph paper and played around with a variety of panel shapes, arranging them in several different permutations to achieve the rhythm I was looking for.

- I used a spirit level and tape measure to draw the shapes on to the walls, following my scale drawing.

- The walls had just been plastered so I used thinned cream emulsion to make them less porous. The watery paint helps to seal the surface.

- I used low-tack masking tape inside the panels to keep my straight lines nice and neat. I made up a rich, dark red using a commercially produced casein (milk-based) paint kit which I tinted with the red oxide provided and applied this to the outside of the panelling. It is not widely accepted that the Romans used this kind of paint, but they certainly used pigments on wet plaster to create the highly durable surface of a fresco.

- Taking a lead from Pompeii, I used a dark green paint to emphasize the inside of some of the panels. This required me to mask out a second square and paint it in the same way.

YOU WILL NEED:

Graph paper
Spirit level
Tape measure
Matt emulsion:
   cream; dark
   green
Low-tack masking
   tape
Casein paint kit
   with red oxide
   pigment

WALL PANELS: LINES AND LASER-COPIED IMAGES

A less extravagant personality might have stopped at the simplistic red, cream and dark green stage of the panelling. I wanted to go further. The Roman love of straight lines meant most of their wall paintings had line upon line within panel upon panel. This kind of straight line painting, or lining as it is known, can be very difficult to pull off. I went for a cheat's solution.

- I created a suitably Roman effect with a selection of coloured, permanent markers and a long ruler.

- For the images inside the panels I made original drawings inspired by some of the best examples of Roman art and laser-copied them on to a special transfer paper.

- I painted pure acrylic over the area where I wished to place each image, and allowed the transfer paper to sit in warm water for one minute until it curled up and the transfer was free from the carrier paper.

- I laid the transfer and paper flat on a piece of newspaper and slid the carrier paper down to expose a couple of centimetres of the back of the transfer. I then pressed the wet transfer on to the pure acrylic and slid the rest of the carrier paper out of the way.

- Finally, I used a squeegee to squeeze out all the water and air.

YOU WILL NEED:

Permanent marker
pens: selection
of colours
Long ruler
Drawings on a
Roman theme
Transfer paper
Pure acrylic (but
PVA will do)
Newspaper
Squeegee
and bucket
of warm
water

THE CEILINGS

Since the Shadrakes' living room was divided in two, the ceilings provided a great opportunity to create a different atmosphere in each area.

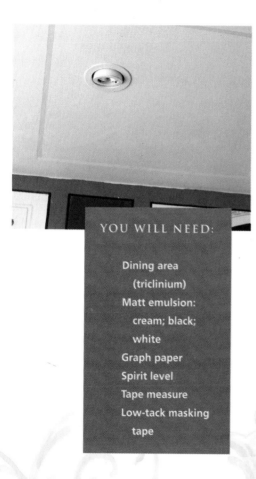

DINING AREA (TRICLINIUM)

I decided to suggest a coffered Roman ceiling by going for trompe-l'oeil panels on a pale background. This was surprisingly easy to achieve.

* I painted the ceiling with cream emulsion.

* I drew the exact layout of the square coffers to a 1:10 scale on graph paper and then marked the coffers out on the ceiling with a spirit level and tape measure. I then drew another line inside each square.

* For the dark and light tones of the ceiling I mixed cream emulsion with black and white emulsion. I applied strips of low-tack masking tape either side of the lines I had drawn around the coffers.

* I used the dark-toned emulsion for the top and side of each coffer and the lighter one for the opposite side and the bottom edge to give the impression of a recessed panel.

ROMAN LIVING ROOM

ATRIUM

I needed a dark ceiling to contrast with the light-reflective panel I had decided to include.

*   I applied a coat of acrylic size to the back of a Perspex panel. When it was sticky and completely clear I rubbed silver transfer leaf on to it with my hand and peeled off the backing paper.

*   Frank used a nail gun to attach plywood boards which had been factory routed to look like tongue-and-groove straight to the ceiling joists.

*   He screwed timber battens on to the plywood to give the feeling of roof joists running around the perimeter of the room. He then fixed two joists across the ceiling into which he fitted the perspex panel. He then added another joist between the long ones to enclose the panel.

*   I applied a few coats of woodstain to the ceiling to darken it down.

YOU WILL NEED:

Watercolours,
including
terracotta, and
the appropriate
brushes
Artist's gouache:
Chinese white
A certain amount
of practice

PAINTED IMAGES

I painted a variety of Roman motifs for the inside of the panels which I later copied and transformed to the wall. Here are a few tips for anyone who wants to paint their own images. Top-quality Roman wall paintings were executed by highly trained Greek slaves who developed a very particular stylistic genre and became masters at working with a technique known as 'painting with the reserve'. This basically means that they used the original colour of the wall to provide the mid-tone between dark shadow and bright highlight.

- Roman walls were often terracotta, so when I had sketched out the basic composition of the motif I wanted, I painted it with a flat wash of terracotta watercolour.

- I painted the motif with watercolours and then gave it a feeling of solidity by using Chinese white artist's gouache to denote where light hit it and dull brown for its shadow.

- I allowed the brush marks to remain obvious – almost like cross hatching – because the Roman technique for fresco did not allow the kind of subtle fading of colour discovered by Renaissance painters.

ROMAN LIVING ROOM

MOSAIC

Anne Schwegmann-Fielding, our mosaic specialist, made the art of mosaic highly accessible with her erudite explanations when she created our mosaic. It reads: *Shadrakae me fecit* (The Shadrakes had me made).

- Anne drew out the design on sketching paper and made a note of the number of small mosaic tiles (tesserae) that were needed to form each element of the pattern. She placed the tiles, face down, in the appropriate areas.

- She stuck ordinary brown paper to the front face of the tesserae using glue so that they formed a large mosaic 'transfer'. She then lifted the entire design and placed it firmly in a bed of tile adhesive.

- When the mosaic had set she soaked the brown paper off with a wet sponge exposing the front face of the tiles.

- She added a little red concrete dye to ready-mixed tile grout to give the pinky glow peculiar to the grout in Roman mosaics and grouted the finished panel.

YOU WILL NEED:

Sketching paper
Mosaic tiles
   (tesserae)
Brown paper
Glue
Tile adhesive
Sponge
Red concrete dye
Ready-mixed tile
   grout

EXPERTS & HELPERS

ANNE SCHWEGMANN-FIELDING
MOSAIC ARTIST

Anne trained as a sculptor but has recently taken up mosaics. She likes recycling and making ordinary objects into beautiful or funny ones. She has exhibited nationally and internationally and won awards for her work. She demonstrated several stages in the process of making a mosaic.

THE SHUTTERS

To cover the wide span of the French windows I used MDF panels, laser-cut with an appropriately Roman design, to make a pair of hinged shutters, one that folded twice and one that folded three times. The shutters created the Roman feel we were looking for and also abolished the modern UPVC window frames.

- I asked Frank to stabilize and strengthen the sometimes delicate fretwork panels with pine battens. He cut each batten to length and routed a groove, the same thickness as the laser-cut MDF, in the middle of it. He then attached battens to the sides of each panel by pushing the fretwork securely into the grooves.

- We used 2 lengths of a 1m (39in) piano hinge per panel to attach each shutter to its neighbour.

- We screwed pine battens into the window reveal and attached large T-hinges to these. The arms of the hinges were then attached to each outermost shutter so that the shutters would 'swing from the wall'.

- I stained the shutters with a dark oak woodstain (MDF takes woodstain in a convincing manner), then gave them a good rub with mahogany-coloured wax to create depth and a slight sheen.

EXPERTS & HELPERS

THE THEOBOLDS BLACKSMITHS

Alan Theobold is seventy-two and has been a blacksmith for most of his life. He shares the business with his son David and grandson John. They used a portable forge and pigskin bellows to demonstrate how a Roman blacksmith might have worked, and made two torcheres and a wall bracket for a hanging lamp from wrought iron. Although we felt that the family trademark of an iron snail wouldn't look quite right in our Roman interior, they presented me with a little hand-worked example which sits on my desk as a momento.

YOU WILL NEED:

Laser-cut fretwork
panels
5 x 2.5cm (2 x 1in)
pine battens
1m (39in) piano
hinges
Large T-hinges
Dark oak
woodstain
Mahogany-
coloured wax

FANTASY ROOMS

FURNITURE

The Shadrakes had several pieces of country pine furniture that could be easily transformed into rugged, rural Roman fixtures.

- I sanded solid pine furniture like the sideboard to remove varnish and wax, then stained the pieces a couple of shades darker than the rather canary shade of the originals.

- Veneered pine pieces were primed with ESP and a brushwood paint effect, available as a two-part kit, was applied.

- I used lead on a roll for suitably Roman bands of metal detailing on rustic pieces. This is normally reserved for 'Tudoring' modern windows and is highly self-adhesive.

- I arranged upholstery tacks in suitable patterns to create a series of convincingly Roman cabinets and couches.

THE LARIUM (HOUSEHOLD SHRINE)

Never be frightened of reincarnating shop-bought packflat furniture. The Shadrakes' extremely ordinary compact disc cabinet had elegant, tall proportions and it struck me that this common or garden cabinet could easily be converted into a typically Roman shrine to the household gods.

Frank used standard architrave mouldings, 18mm (¾in) MDF and a Roman frame of mind to create a temple-esque upper cabinet. When this was fixed on top of the original cabinet it conveyed the architectural solidity and classical serenity of a fifth century AD domestic shrine.

YOU WILL NEED:

Sandpaper
Woodstain
ESP
Brushwood paint
    effect kit
Lead on a roll
Upholstery tacks

CURTAIN TREATMENT

I called to mind the rough, woven fabrics of the Roman era by using hessian as the major soft furnishing statement. Hanging these homespun draperies from a contemporary curtain pole would have been at odds with the Shadrakes' vision, and Frank cunningly hit upon the idea of using a copper pipe and hanging it from cup hooks that had been screwed into the wall.

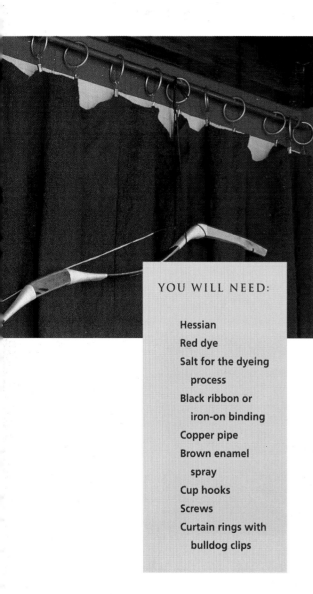

YOU WILL NEED:

Hessian

Red dye

Salt for the dyeing
    process

Black ribbon or
    iron-on binding

Copper pipe

Brown enamel
    spray

Cup hooks

Screws

Curtain rings with
    bulldog clips

- We dyed hessian with a red machine dye and made it into curtains which would act as a room divider. I used black ribbon for a double black band at the bottom hems – yet more Roman straight lines which also incidentally found their way on to mattress covers and cushions – but iron-on binding will do just as well and is quick to apply.

- I sprayed a length of a plumber's copper pipe with a patchy coat of brown enamel to transform this everyday object, giving it an authentic look of rusting iron.

- Frank screwed cup hooks into the wall and hung the pole from them. Because the hooks bend quite a long way back on themselves, they literally grip the pipe in place.

- I used steel-effect curtain rings and bulldog clips to hold the curtains. OK, so the Romans hadn't invented the bulldog clip – but I'm sure that if they had, they would have used it.

FUR-COVERED CAMPAIGN STOOLS

I had never seen a house with so much fur in it – much of it attached to the Shadrakes' huge dogs. Any self-respecting late centurion would have amassed a cuddly collection of fur pelts to warm his retirement in chilly Britain. Shelve political correctness for a moment: fake fur is not only a good way of creating that late Roman Empire feel, it is also one of the most talked about interior fashion accessories of the late twentieth century. I use it a lot in my more sumptuous schemes, as an edging for bed throws, a detail on curtains or just for the hell of it. Our very military-looking campaign stools were especially successful as Roman make-believe, and even took in Paul Sealey, our Roman expert, before he had a chance to study them carefully.

- I bought cheap director's chairs and disassembled the arms and back of each, leaving just half a chair – exactly like a Roman folding seat.

- I cut nylon bear fur fabric into the approximate shapes of pelts with pinking shears, and draped them over the chairs.

YOU WILL NEED:

Director's chairs
Fake fur
Pinking shears

THE PRODUCTS

I used the following products for the Roman living room.

ROMAN WALL PANELS

Graph paper. Stationers.
Dulux matt emulsion: Georgian Cream
Crown matt emulsion: dark green (Mishima 53/80)
Nutshell casein paint mixed with red oxide pigment
Easimask low-tack masking tape. Brewers

WALL PANELS: THE LINES AND LASER-COPIED IMAGES

Pantone pens 13, 139, 484, 3292. London Graphic Centre
Roman motifs from a source book
Lazertran paper. Mail order
Pure acrylic or PVA. Art shops
Newspaper

THE CEILINGS

Dining area (*triclinium*)
Graph paper. Stationers
Dulux matt emulsion: Georgian cream; black; white
Easimask low-tack masking tape. Brewers

ATRIUM

Perspex panel, cut to size. DIY stores
Acrylic Wundasize. London Graphic Centre; good art shops
Silver transfer leaf. Cornelissen
Schauman WISA-decor routed plyboards. Travis Perkins

10 x 5cm (4 x 2in) timber battens. DIY stores
Dulux Weathershield Aquatech Woodstain: dark oak

PAINTED IMAGES

Watercolours. Art shops
Artist's gouache: Chinese white. London Graphic Centre

THE MOSAIC

Sketching paper
Mosaic tiles (tesserae). Ask at your local tile shop
Tile adhesive. DIY stores
Red concrete dye. DIY stores
Ready-mixed tile grout. DIY stores

SHUTTERS

'Jupiter' fretwork panels. Jali
5 x 2.5cm (2 x 1in) pine battens. DIY stores
Piano hinges. DIY stores
Large T-hinges. DIY stores
Dulux Weathershield Aquatech Woodstain: dark oak
Liberon Black Bison fine paste wax: Georgian mahogany

FURNITURE

ESP. Ray Munn
Dulux Brushwood Twin Pack paint effect kit
Lead on a roll. Lead & Light; Homebase
Upholstery tacks. DIY stores

CURTAIN TREATMENT

Hessian. John Lewis
Dylon machine dye: red. DIY stores and haberdashery departments/stores
Black ribbon. John Lewis or: Bondaweb iron-on binding. Haberdashery departments/stores
Copper pipe. DIY stores
Plasti-Kote Nut Brown Enamel Spray. DIY stores
Cup hooks. DIY stores
'Adele' bulldog-clip curtain rings. IKEA

FUR-COVERED CAMPAIGN STOOLS

Director's chairs. The Pier
Fake bear fur. Epra
Fake wolf fur. Broadwick Silks

GENERAL

Plain pine beds. Thuhra International, available in Argos catalogue: No. 645/4344
Pots. Classic Pot Emporium
Cushion pads. John Lewis
Small terracotta Roman lamps. British Museum Shop
Candles. Angelic, Neal Street branch.
Celtic Knot solar-powered fountain. Solar Solutions Fountains

CHAPTER 4
HEAVENLY

BED
ROOM

MOST PEOPLE'S FANTASY ROOMS are about escaping from mundane life, and in many ways the ultimate fantasy is to set out to achieve heaven. The specifics of heaven change from period to period, culture to culture, continent to continent. To the ancient Egyptians the afterlife was pragmatically after life – everything continued as before. Debts were sometimes recorded as being payable only after death; and tomb paintings abound with comic-strip depictions of normal life as pharaohs hobnob with the gods. The Greeks employed a two-tier approach to survival after death. Great heroes hung out on the Elysian Fields, energetically showing off their athletic capabilities to appreciative deities. They were most assuredly flying business class. Ordinary souls were offered neither increased leg room nor blankets to keep out the chill winds of Hades. Christianity, when it emerged, focused on the promise of living in a state of eternal bliss, as compared to the sacrifices demanded in life and irrelevance of material possessions.

My original design for Joni's heaven.

More personally, the most wholly, the most entirely and uncompromisingly subjective concept for any of us has to be our view of heaven. And in this world, on a practical level, Joni Donoghue's idea of heaven is a heavenly bedroom, where she can indulge her love of all things holistic and spiritual. When I first heard that heaven was to be our theme I could not get images of pink fluffy clouds and comforting angel wings out of my mind. Indeed, although these specific elements became abstracted in the final scheme there still remained the strong flavour of a colourful and a rather innocent vision of heaven.

FANTASY ROOMS

PARADISE AND ANGELS

The heaven of Christian and Jewish belief – like the Islamic paradise – has always been the ultimate reward for those who have followed the path laid down by their religion. And regardless of their faith, there has always been someone to tell them that existence was such and should be conducted in such a way; and that if it was, they would progress to a very particular state. In fact in the Christian tradition, there was always as much information about hell as there was about heaven.

Islam was always more optimistic. The specific architecture of Paradise was documented (Muslims are not allowed to depict either Allah or heaven pictorially) and carefully catalogued. The highly cultivated Moors designed their exquisitely shaded interior gardens to include exact scale models of the four rivers of Paradise.

These typical Renaissance cherubs (believe it or not) started life in the Old Testament, described as wheels of fire. The route from pre-classical spinning fireball to post-classical winged toddler is a tortuous one. (Painting by Andrea Mantegna.)

THE REVEREND
CANON KEITH WALKER

Canon Walker is the education officer at Winchester Cathedral, which houses the unique Chapel of the Guardian Angels. He told us about the angelic hierarchy of nine orders of angels in the Bible. We talked about what guardian angels are and what they mean, as well as why angels have been depicted in particular ways in art through the ages. Many people believe that angels take on human form and visit earth specifically to protect individuals – and many firmly believe that they have been visited by their guardian angel. Canon Walker holds true to the Christian perception that angels are totally spiritual, not human in form or action; and that heaven is a spiritual, not physical, place – a new dimension full of 'light, love and joy'.

While making this television series I asked the same question of the individuals we visited, often when the cameras were turned off. I asked each of them for their own personal description of what they thought heaven would be like. Some suggested that we all have to undergo a few more incarnations to achieve nirvana; but all agreed that heaven or paradise – or whatever – meant being included in some form of divine energy. Canon Walker of Winchester Cathedral also admitted to looking forward to being reunited with his much lamented and recently departed cat, Sophie.

Angels are the messengers of heaven and most of us still seem to hold a sugar-coated place in our hearts for the radiantly vacuous, shiningly blond hermaphrodites that hover over sleeping, curly-haired infants in Victorian moralistic engravings. It is fascinating that every culture has flying beings – just as every culture has dragons. For an explanation of this universality of angels it is necessary to dig into our cultural past. An engrossing, but by no means totally accepted, view centres on the role and function of ancient priests or shaman whose primary function was to act as intermediaries between earth and heaven. Textbook angels. To do this, a shaman was expected to achieve the gift of flight and literally commute between the two states.

Angels, as we recognize them, have their sculptural forebears in ancient Greece. The androgyne spreading its large, comforting wings over fluttering drapery is not far removed from statues depicting Nike, goddess of victory. Later, small winged figures started appearing on vases. When I say small, I literally mean miniature, fully grown humans with the wingspan of an albatross. Although they often cropped up with Aphrodite, goddess of love, they were not necessarily her son Eros but were more probably the winged souls of recently departed heroes.

Comfort comes from the caress of angelic arms or wings, even in this classical painting with its unstated erotic subtext. (Francois Gerard)

JONI DONOGHUE
AND HER VISION

Joni Donoghue is a self-employed mother of two young daughters, Jazzula and Blaize, and three cats. They all live in a large Victorian terraced house in Brighton, which she is in the process of renovating. Her big passions are astrology, tarot and all things spiritual but, because of work demands, she had very little time to indulge them. In spite of her commitment to the more ethereal concepts of existence, she is immensely practical and down to earth. She is studying computing and is in the process of setting up another business selling recycling equipment. She has a very strong and confident personality and talks with educated knowledge about her interests.

In conversation we shared many of our points of reference for heaven. Joni's interests, however, brought other influences, many of which I had never encountered, into the melting pot. Her vision of how her fantasy could be achieved included elements from a variety of New Age philosophies such as Feng Shui, tarot, crystals and astrology. As we explored them it was amazing how quickly some of them began to feel rather comfortingly familiar. There was no doubt that, for Joni, heaven is firmly non-denominational and – bearing in mind her passion for the Brighton sunset – elemental.

Her fantasy was at first very difficult to understand, mainly because English lacks so many appropriate words for states of mind. However, her strength of character and her confidence in following her own path meant that she was more than prepared to accept some quite theatrical, knowingly clichéd elements, which more than satisfied my desire to provide them. A heaven full of monotonous chanting and clicking beads would be hell to turn into an interior.

Joni talked a lot about heaven but she also talked a lot about angels and guardian angels in particular. She and I shared certain preconceptions, and we discussed them and honed for ourselves a shopping list of elements that we found either spiritual or aesthetic. Joni then introduced me to a series of what I can only call disciplines, which offer contrasting ladders that allow the believer to scale the heights of heaven. All the practitioners I met were engaging, modest and thoroughly modern. Each was able to demonstrate a highly charismatic flexibility seemingly at odds with perceived orthodoxy – and at Winchester Cathedral Canon Walker took me aback with his accessible message and off-beat humour.

At the end of the twentieth century, many of us are groping our way blindfold through a maze of contrasts, blind alleys and too many spiritual choices. A smart man, I suppose, takes the best from all. A smart man uses many subjective viewpoints to achieve his own objective stance. In this instance, a smart man decided to paint horizontal bands. Interior decoration got the better of my theology and getting Joni's bedroom to feel like heaven was going to be something of a difficult aesthetic labour.

CHRIS AND THE FALLEN ANGEL

The Fallen Angel is a bookshop and New Age shop in Lewes that sells all sorts of fascinating things and also operates a mail order service for the practice of white magic. It is owned and run by Chris, who has been a practising white witch for over twenty years and is now high priest of his coven. Joni is a great fan of his shop and took me there to illustrate the atmosphere she wanted to achieve in her own earthly heaven. Chris attributes her love for his shop to the fact that she was a witch in a previous existence. Joni herself remains unconvinced.

105

MY FIRST REACTION TO THE SPACE

Joni's bedroom sits at the top of a tall house on top of a tall hill. Through the window there is only sky – a sky which apparently provides her with spectacularly lit celestial sunsets. The fireplace is off centre on the wall, creating unequal spaces on either side. By Joni's own admission, the room was horribly cluttered.

I found the inclusion into the scheme of a feng shui appraisal a challenge. The relationship corner had been found on a diagonal to the door and would have to be left embellished but unhindered. Because the bed lived in the middle of the room it was 'floating' and therefore needed to be 'anchored', and the colour scheme should be predominantly pink, accessorized with vases of white chrysanthemums. Now, I loved the idea of a floating bed and it seemed to me that this was exactly what Joni wanted. We eventually compromised by leaving the bed where it was but anchoring it to the ceiling with gilded ropes. Neither of us could bring ourselves to love pinks, so I suggested we take the prettiness of Barbie pink through to butch lilacs, and beyond to ultramarine. The darkness of the darkest blue would highlight the paleness and luminosity of the pinks.

I thought it would be best to provide the unequal spaces left by the chimney breast with low-level cupboards and an MDF surround to reduce the void between the face of the chimney breast and the back of the apertures.

A soft cream, almost shagpile carpet could pass for a fluffy white cloud if Joni closed her eyes. It struck me as being important to provide as many sensory experiences

as possible. More than anything, it should be the ultimate indulgence that would allow a mother of two small daughters to be away from the constant demands of home life, and as far removed as possible from her office telephone and fax. It had to be the interior equivalent of a warm, bubbly bath, a cold, bracing country walk or a solitary hot chocolate.

The heaven I tried to create for Joni is a heaven of contrasts, where the lightness of light is best illustrated next to the darkness of dark. The broad horizontal bands darken from floor to ceiling in an effort to encompass Joni's beloved heavenly sunsets within her personal paradise. The bands, as well as prosaically making the room appear much bigger, also allude to a self-imposed constraint adopted by both of us. We could not create a scheme that tried to show all of heaven – there had to be some mystery, there had to be some allowance for personal perception.

Broad horizontal bands are excellent camouflage. I can't imagine that heaven is centrally heated, it almost certainly doesn't have wardrobes and even the door to heaven felt odd because it was four-panelled. So we flung the horizontal bands over everything that didn't move and perspective played the

EXPERTS & HELPERS

EVE PEACOCK
FENG SHUI EXPERT

Feng shui is about the flow of 'chi' or creative energy, which should be as unhindered and therefore as positive as possible in a room. Eve has been a practitioner for three years. She started giving tarot and psychic readings at the age of twenty-eight and these led her to this ancient Chinese art. She was also taught palmistry by a famous Indian practitioner. There are different types of feng shui and Eve practises the most common form: Black Hat. It originated in New York and is founded on the belief that all energies in a room come through the door and that the correct layout of a room depends on how areas relate to the door's position.

Eve quickly identified the problems in Joni's bedroom and I tried to work round them while remaining faithful to the design elements which I knew to be important to Joni as well as to me. Eve came to check the room out when we had finished and generally seemed to approve of our interpretation of her original feng shui specification.

most extraordinary tricks – we literally lost a rather bulky, 1930s wardrobe into the wall. You could still tell it was there only by the gilded handles. This amused me enormously: why not deconstruct the heavenly effect there and then with an absurd subversive element? The randomly configured candle shelves positioned over the fireplace did this a treat, as did the fireplace itself left hanging against the sky.

It was at this point that I started to think of René Magritte, the Belgian surrealist painter. His vision included railway locomotives, mermaids that are fish from the belly button up and ordinary working men in bowler hats whose faces are replaced by apples or who commonly float, unhindered, in a blue fluffy clouded sky.

Trying to be bold about using cliché, I felt manly specifying organza at the window. Although there was no way either Joni or I would go as far as actually pearlizing some wrought-iron gates, heaven seemed to insist on gauzy, filmy draperies. Heaven also relied heavily on candlelight for illumination. This element dovetailed with the spiritual significance of candles, which our experts had often stressed. The crystal bead curtains at the windows were a bit of old nonsense, but surprisingly effective if you remember their humble nativity as cheap Christmas tree decorations.

The highly emotive spread of an angel's wings from the pen of the great nineteenth-century illustrator, Gustave Doré, is difficult to strike from your memory. The British artist William Blake knew how to stylize them so that they became as powerful, yet decorative, as Gothic tracery. And angels' wings

are a universal hieroglyph that means comfort and protection. Joni's bed needed comforting, nurturing and protective wings to guard her head at night. I was desperate that the bed should appear to hover (a rather over-clever sideways reference to the flight of the shaman). Eve Peacock, the hugely erudite feng shui consultant, remained adamant that it should be firmly anchored. I liked the idea of anchoring it to heaven rather than earth so that the whole bed would appear to be in the process of assisted levitation rather than heavy, encumbered almost-flight.

Joni and I had taken in and digested angels from Coptic to contemporary, belief systems from the most rigid to the most 'organic'; and we had explored heaven from as many viewpoints as we could find in a wet week in Brighton. Joni's real fantasy – which I tried to fulfil – was to be that ordinary person who could, at will, should they want to, leave their feet of clay behind and ascend to a heavenly plane, free from the mundane banalities of existence.

HEAVenly BEDroom THE PROJects

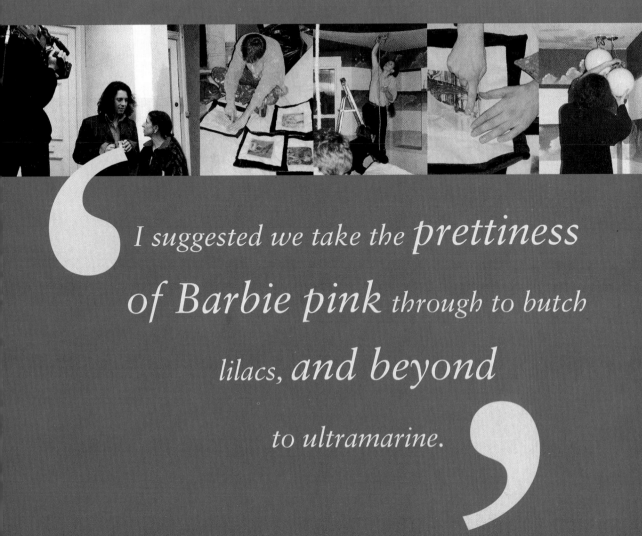

I suggested we take the prettiness of Barbie pink through to butch lilacs, and beyond to ultramarine.

WALL BANDS

It's not just an old wives' tale that horizontal stripes make things broader and vertical stripes make them longer. If you need a lot of help with the dimensions of your room, the greater the contrast between the stripes the more pronounced the effect will be.

YOU WILL NEED:

Matt emulsion:
  pink; dark pink;
  lilac; dark lilac;
  ultramarine;
  pale grey; pale
  cream
Spirit level
7.5cm (3in)
  low-tack
  masking tape
Purple universal
  paint stainer
Acrylic scumble
  glaze
Brushes, including
  a 5cm (2in)
  brush and
  medium artist's
  brush

- We painted the room with cream emulsion. I measured the walls and decided to allow myself four painted bands which I drew using a spirit level to check the line. As I went along I masked the bands with low-tack masking tape to ensure a nice clean edge.

- For the sky colours on the bands I chose pink, dark pink, lilac, dark lilac and ultramarine emulsions. On Joni's suggestion I added some purple universal paint stainer to enrich and warm the ultramarine. To each of the colours I added approximately one-third again of acrylic scumble glaze. This meant I could paint one colour at the bottom of a band and a different one at the top and have enough time to merge the two with horizontal strokes of a dry brush before the paints dried.

- To achieve delicate, transparent clouds I added a little pale grey emulsion to acrylic scumble glaze and used a 5cm (2in) brush to roughly block in the shapes of the clouds while the paint was still wet.

- Using a medium artist's brush I highlighted the clouds with pale cream emulsion straight from the tin to give the effect of the sun catching them from behind. I softened some of the lines with a dry brush and left others as more atmospheric highlights.

STARS FOR THE WALL BANDS

When I was at college we were taught never to use white straight from the tube. It was only ever to be mixed with other colours. There is truth in this and I keep pure white for a special treat – which is painting stars.

Believe it or not, white comes in a variety of colours. Flake white is pinky, zinc white is yellow and titanium white, being bluey, is the most powerful of all.

- To give Joni's stars luminescence, I diluted the cream emulsion I had used for the cloud highlights with water and sprayed random patches on to the wall through an old-fashioned mouth diffuser.

- In the centre of each aura I painted a simple star using titanium white acrylic straight from the tube. Because the stars are the only note of true white in a room that is all cream, ultramarine or shades of sunset, they really do appear to shine.

YOU WILL NEED:

Matt emulsion:
pale cream
Mouth diffuser
and plenty of
puff
Artist's acrylic
colour: titanium
white

VELVET THROW

The pale-coloured bed would have looked
lost in the room without an accent of
darkness, so we made a simple but
luxurious bed throw.

- I lined a square of dark navy velvet with navy
  satin. For added sparkle, lengths of crystal
  bead edging were handstitched to the edges.

YOU WILL NEED:

Dark navy cotton
velvet
Navy satin lining
Crystal bead
edging

HEAVENLY BED

The wings at the head of the bed were laser-cut out of MDF to my design. A slightly less high-tech solution would be to use a jigsaw if you're prepared to cut around all those feathers.

- Frank built a timber-slatted bed frame about 20cm (8 in) high and then made a box from 18mm (¾in) MDF. He screwed the box to the floor and attached the bed frame to the box. The frame overhangs the box so from most angles the bed appears to be floating.

- I put a delicately moulded pine cornice around the base of the bed frame and used satinwood cream paint for it and the footboard. I applied a base coat of cream paint to the wings and attached them at the head end. Picking up on the gloriously multicoloured wings of angels in pre-Renaissance art, I used three subtle, pearlescent acrylic colours to softly delineate the feathers. I allowed plenty of the cream base coat to show through between the painted feathers.

- In accordance with instructions from our feng shui expert, we anchored the bed with four lengths of rope. We gilded these with gold enamel spray then wrapped flexible wire tightly around them and looped the wire around screws driven into appropriate places on the bed and ceiling.

YOU WILL NEED:

Timber planks for
the bed frame
18mm (¾in) MDF
for the box and
wings
Screws
MDF for the
footboard, cut
to shape
Moulded pine
cornice
Satinwood paint:
pale cream
Pearlescent acrylic
colours: violet;
blue; pink
Ropes
Gold enamel spray
Flexible wire

HEAVENLY BEDROOM

ANGEL CHAIRS

It is important to use chairs made from untreated timber because otherwise you will have to sand and prepare them. As with the heavenly bed, the wings were laser-cut to my design. The covering for the chairs is made from the same fabrics as the velvet throw.

- For each chair, Frank attached the wings to its sides with screws. I painted both the chair and wings cream and applied the same feathery details that were used for the headboard to the wings with pearlescent acrylic colours.

- A length of foam rubber was cut to fit over the chair, from the top of the back to just above the bottom of the legs. Dark navy velvet was sewn to the front of the foam and a lining of navy satin to the back.

- For a really neat look I secured the covering to the back of the top chair rail with Velcro.

- For a finishing touch I attached a couple of lovely, opulent gold tassels to the bottom corners of the covering. I made these from several shades of gold-coloured wool which I cut to a uniform length and divided into two bundles. I then wrapped wool in a contrasting colour around each bundle, about a quarter of the way from the top.

YOU WILL NEED:

2 chairs made from
    untreated timber
18mm (¾in) MDF
    for the wings
Screws
Satinwood paint:
    pale cream
Pearlescent acrylic
    colours: violet;
    blue; pink
2.5cm (1in)
    fire-retardant
    foam rubber
Dark navy cotton
    velvet
Navy satin lining
Velcro
Gold-coloured
    wool to make
    your own
    tassels, or 2 big
    gold tassels

WINDOW TREATMENT

For a large proportion of the year our windows are filled with cold and uninviting northern light. On the bright side, there's plenty of it. Filtering this strong but chilly light through cream-coloured muslin has been one of the decorating successes of the past few years. But trends in interior design being what they are, this season's muslin is organza. Real organza is a translucent, transiently coloured, gossamer-thin silk with a nice stiffness to it. There are now plenty of accessible and affordable fakes. Used simply, hung from bulldog-clip curtain rings, it has a filmy delicacy and glorious modernity. Joni threaded bells which she found in a junk shop through the clips.

YOU WILL NEED:

Organza
Iron-on bonding
for hems
Curtain
Bulldog-clip
curtain rings
Bells

CUSHION COVERS

Making the cushion covers involves using image transfer which transfers the coloured powders that make up the image of a laser copy on to fabric, and fixes it there permanently. The transferred images have to be left overnight for the process to 'take'.

- We made several simple envelope-style cushion covers for 40cm (16in) cushion pads. Each cover consisted of a 7.5cm (3in) border of dark navy velvet surrounding a square panel of pale cream canvas.

- Joni and I chose a selection of angel parts from a variety of postcards from the National Gallery – a wing here, an arm there, a fold of flowing nightie in the middle – and laser-copied them. We then used image transfer to apply them to the canvas squares.

- We left the covers overnight and then removed the paper, which had now become backing paper, by rubbing gently with a damp cloth. In their final state the transferred images were rather pleasingly antiqued like a Renaissance fresco, but be warned – removing the backing paper takes a lot of rubbing.

YOU WILL NEED:

Cushion pads
Dark navy cotton
velvet
Cream duck canvas
Laser copies of
angel images
Image transfer

YOU WILL NEED:

Globe lights with
brass chains

LIGHT-FITTINGS

For once in unquestioning accordance with feng shui, I knew that the central light-fitting directly above Joni's tummy as she lay in bed didn't fit. I find that the best and most successful way to approach lighting in any room is to illuminate the corners with low-level lights rather than installing a central, bright, morgue light just underneath the ceiling. When tackling electrical work of the complexity involved in this project it is important to employ the skills of a qualified electrician.

- A handful of illuminated orbs wouldn't go amiss in a heavenly bedroom, so I asked the electrician to run additional light points to the ceiling in diagonally opposite corners of the room and to arrange the points in clusters of three.

- He connected globe lights made from opaque glass to the points and I varied their heights by removing or adding the links in their brass chains.

CANDLE SHELVES

I loved the way the wall bands were working, travelling over radiators, wardrobes, doors and any other architectural feature in a rather Magritte-ish kind of way. To heighten this subtext of surrealism, I thought it would be fun to subvert the trompe-l'oeil sky I had created by attaching surprising elements to the wall on top of the stripes. We wanted plenty of places to put church candles so Frank made some small shelves for them.

- Frank cut chunky blocks out of rough pine shelving and fixed them discreetly to the wall with concealed brackets. It took ages for us to work out a random enough pattern for the shelves – as symmetrical beings we find asymmetry difficult to relate to.

- I gilded the blocks roughly, allowing the pronounced grain of the pine to come through the acrylic size and gold transfer leaf.

YOU WILL NEED:

5cm (2in) pine
shelving
Concealed
brackets
Acrylic gold size
Gold transfer leaf

CRYSTAL BEAD CURTAINS

Inspired by our meeting with a crystal expert, I decided to replace Joni's tired net curtains with a fabulous shimmering bead one. This device, known in the eighteenth century as a 'glass curtain', is more than successful at preventing people seeing in – and also casts celestial shadows and heavenly rainbows. To filter the light and add a further element of privacy, I hung cream roller blinds behind the glass curtain.

- I attached roller blinds to the underside of the top window frame.

- I used screws and Rawlplugs to attach timber battens that had been cut to the width of the windows to the wall just below the ceiling. I then cut lengths of translucent plastic Christmas decoration beads to fit from the top of the battens to the floor.

- I bound florist's wire tightly around the topmost bead on each length and wound the wire several times around the batten to hold it in place.

YOU WILL NEED:

Cream roller blinds
Timber battens
Screws and
    Rawlplugs
Lengths of
    pearlescent
    beads
Florist's wire (or
    any other
    flexible wire)

THE PRODUCTS

I used the following products for the heavenly bedroom.

WALL BANDS

Dulux matt emulsion: ultramarine (50BB 10/182)

Johnstone's matt emulsion: (E15-32; E15-34; E1-2; E2-22)

7.5cm (3in) Easimask low-tack masking tape. Brewers

Purple universal paint stainer. Art shops

Polyvine Scumble Glaze. DIY stores

STARS FOR THE WALL BANDS

Crown Paints matt emulsion: Antique Cream (C1-10)

Daler Rowney mouth diffuser

Artist's acrylic colour: titanium white

VELVET THROW

Dark navy cotton velvet. Broadwick Silks

Navy satin lining. John Lewis

Crystal bead edging. VV Rouleaux

HEAVENLY BED

Timber planks for the bed frame. Timber merchants

18mm (¾in) MDF for the box and wings. DIY stores

MDF headboard. Laser-cut by Jali

Richard Burbidge moulded pine cornice. Homebase

Crown Paints satinwood: Antique Cream (C1-10)

Pearlescent acrylic colours: violet; blue; pink. Daler Rowney

Ropes. Hardware stores

Plasti-Kote Gold Enamel Spray. DIY stores

Flexible wire. Hardware stores

ANGEL CHAIRS

2 x 'Ivar' chairs. IKEA

18mm (¾in) MDF for the wings. DIY stores

Crown Paints satinwood: Antique Cream (C1-10)

Pearlescent acrylic colours: violet; blue; pink. Daler Rowney

2.5cm (1in) fire-retardant foam rubber. Pentonville Rubber

Dark navy cotton velvet. Broadwick Silks

Navy satin lining. John Lewis

Velcro. Haberdashery departments/shops

Gold-coloured wool for tassels. John Lewis or: 2 big gold tassels. Haberdashery departments/stores

WINDOW TREATMENT

Gold organza. Nasar Collections

Bondaweb iron-on bonding for hems. Haberdashery departments/shops

12mm (½in) copper pipe. DIY stores

'Adele' bulldog-clip curtain rings. IKEA

CUSHION COVERS

Polyester cushion pads. John Lewis

Dark navy cotton velvet. Broadwick Silks

Cream 7½oz duck canvas. Wolfin Textiles

Laser copies of angel images; we used a set of postcards from the National Gallery © The National Gallery

Dylon Image Maker. John Lewis

LIGHT-FITTINGS

Globe lights with brass chains. Homebase

CANDLE SHELVES

5cm (2in) pine shelving. Homebase

Concealed brackets. DIY stores

Acrylic Wundasize. London Graphic Centre

Gold transfer leaf. London Graphic Centre

CRYSTAL BEAD CURTAINS

Cream roller blinds. IKEA

5 x 2.5cm (2 x 1in) timber battens. DIY stores

Rolls of pearlescent beads. DZD

GENERAL

Table. IKEA

Candles. Angelic

Plastic plant dishes. Hardware stores

Hanging lamps. Homebase

Angel sculpture: 'Fame' by John Michael Rysbreach. Donated by V & A Enterprises

Gold leaf picture frames. Homebase

Moderna carpet: Wild Pearl (04/6446]. Kingsmead Carpets

CHAPTER 5

SEVENTIES

DINING
ROOM

The last quarter of the twentieth century has given rise to an extraordinary phenomenon – the revival of the styles our parents swore by. The early 1970s saw a 1950s revival. The early 1980s saw a 1960s revival. And in the 1990s what could be more natural than a Seventies revival? To me the era means hessian walls, white laminate, room-dividers and huge smoked-glass cubes that hovered between being art objects and ceiling lights. It was the age of installations and happenings, the time when artists and designers discovered contemporary materials like plastics and Perspex. It was also, in the words of Chris Sykes, the decade of 'dodgy haircuts and flares'. This aside, the Seventies strikes a chord with Chris. To him it is a high-energy, glamour-friendly era – unlike the Nineties – and his fantasy is to create the ultimate 1970s dining room.

A dining room fit for a King - Jason King that is.

THE SEVENTIES

Although I was more than old enough to experience and appreciate the Seventies I missed out on the decade. With hindsight, my upbringing had a curiously pre-war feel to it. But I vividly remember how some of my parents' friends lived. In particular, one incredibly chic couple moved into an enormous Victorian rectory and removed every trace of nineteenth-

century Gothicary from the interior architecture. Their large, airy, open-plan 'living space' seemed to be part of the brave new world of design.

Everything inside the house was sleek, uninterrupted, ergonomically conceived to save space (a weird anomaly in what was an enormous building) and, above all, designed to abolish the right-angled corner. I was impressed. It was to me, at the age of ten, the largest, most concerted, most emphatically seductive piece of uncompromising design I had ever seen. I realize now that in inspiration, in feeling, it was as powerful, as emphatic, as the baroque architecture of Jules Mansart in France in the 1670s, the neoclassical buildings designed by Robert Adam in the 1770s or the Gothic Revival style of William Morris in the 1870s. It was a planet apart from the self-deprecating chintzes and good-tempered but unremarkable antiques of my childhood home. It was frightfully un-British and, for that, I loved it.

Design never happens in a vacuum. It grows from the ethos of a particular time, an ethos that is sometimes political and often economic and which changes with society itself. Just as the Seventies house that I admired so much at the age of ten reflected the decade's fascination with all things technological, so Modernism, the major design movement of the twentieth century, reflected a widespread rejection of traditional forms of artistic expression – in particular, those of the nineteenth century. For the Modernist architects and designers of the 1920s, building was about intellect, about function and integrity of materials and principally

about the abolition of ornament. The movement initially had very little impact on domestic buildings in Britain, however, and throughout the 1930s building styles were essentially revisionist. People bought – hook, line and sinker – the comforting nostalgia of Sir Edwin Lutyens and other suburban architects who followed.

The Second World War changed all that. If the Great War had been about manpower, its later cousin was about harnessing technology for its full destructive potential. Inevitably, life was never going to be the same again when the war ended. Society had come to the brink, had looked down into the hideous abyss of

The integrated multi-functional living unit.

self-destruction and somehow the cosy redbrick cocoon of suburbia had lost its comfort and appeal. Not only had the war destroyed many of the nation's homes, it had also bankrupted it, making it impossible to rebuild Britain in expensive, ornamental, historicized brick. Concrete was basically all we could afford but more than that, after the hideousness of conflict, modernist concrete was all that we felt we really deserved.

So the design landscape of Britain which for 400 years had been about slow, subtle aesthetic changes was suddenly disfigured with abrupt, prosthetic structures that were all about use and not about beauty. The British are a pragmatic people and actually managed to convince themselves that Modernism was a good thing. They flocked to the Festival of Britain in 1951. They hardboarded over Victorian panelled doors, ripped out ornate fireplaces and revelled in the fact that they had radically reduced the total surface area that required dusting in a room.

1950s Modernism became 1960s Mod(ernism). Lines became cleaner, shapes became simpler and ornament faded out altogether. By the late Sixties the vision of technology as the fifth horseman of the apocalypse had largely faded (although CND stuck like the Ancient Mariner to its nuclear-powered guns), to be replaced by the spectacular reality of men landing on the moon. Thus everything went space age – the future had arrived and the future was plastic.

The 1970s was the decade that went through three major redefinitions of taste. The first really started in the late Sixties and developed from optimism in the future, from the application of technology for the visual betterment of mankind. Its designers loved to offer a multitude of uses for a single piece of furniture and this was the era of the 'integrated living machine' (front room), 'multipurpose eating facility' (dining room) and the 'dormition bubble' (circular bed). They drew inspiration from the conceptual

intellectualized art movements of the New York scene. Art installations had just come to the fore and were instantly turned into interior design. Pop Art, Op Art, Abstract Expressionism, Kinetic Art, Found Art all came together as unlikely but nevertheless stylish window treatments or tableware.

For a style obsessed with both technology and plastic, the oil crisis of 1973/74 spelt terminal disaster, adding impetus to the underground hippy ecology of the 1960s which had fled from technology into the open arms and unsupported bosom of homespun earthmotherdom. Overnight, white, extruded plastic drinking vessels became hideously heavy chocolate-brown and orange mugs. Sleek and sexy chromed bubble chairs were replaced by pitched pine pews and the appropriately named shag-pile carpet was reborn as scritchy-scratchy sisal or, worse, cork tiles. Where brightly coloured kinetic art objects had once hung, macramé plant pots dangled holding a legion of flaccid spider plants. The stage had been set for the insidious spread of the Dralon couch, wallpaper border and stripped-pine door frame.

In the late 1970s, following the lead of Richard Rogers, the decade's third style developed. It exposed ducts on the exteriors of buildings, supported beds on scaffolding poles, and called itself hi-tech – which says it all. Design no longer belonged to the people, who found this latest development unsympathetic. It was something that only the elite or the hopelessly socially advantaged pursued. Architects loved it for their own houses, the intelligentsia adored it for its subliminal recognition of the punk movement but everybody else ignored it. What's more, they ignored everything that followed – a nation that had accepted design as a part of life since the mid-Forties suddenly decided to reinvent itself as a race of conservative, anti-design Philistines.

It is not surprising that a new generation takes one look at the woolly present and is repulsed. And that, in its repulsion, it finds itself pushed by some invisible force back to the days when parties 'swung', when music throbbed to a disco beat and Abba ruled the waves.

Sleek living has no room for right angles.

CHRIS SYKES AND HIS VISION

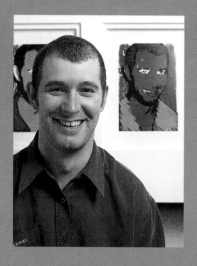

Chris Sykes lives in a neat Victorian terraced house in Stockport, outside Manchester. He is a car mechanic which probably comes in handy since his pride and joy is his bright yellow 1971 Volkswagen camper van – complete with a fittingly Seventies interior and a stack of Abba CDs on the dashboard – which he takes to VW meetings all over the country. As a child of the Sixties he lived through the Seventies and loves the connotations of 'groovy' and the appeal of the 'tacky'.

Like me, Chris grew up with those incredibly sexy 'lifestyle' sets television designers cobbled together for that great Seventies television institution, *Play for Today*. Trouser-suited actresses smoking Rothman's Regals failed to convince as bored, lonely housewives while moustachioed graphic designers or City brokers in paisley caftans played the part of errant husbands. Marriage traumas were enacted against a backdrop of curvilinear room-dividers, large abstract paintings and perpetually stocked drinks cabinets. The denouement often left one or even both of the protagonists dead on the white shag-pile, culled by a heavy glass ashtray. I'm not sure that anyone really did decorate their houses with such cavalier and ultimately seductive taste, but the fiction was compulsive.

Both Chris and I also remember the sheer adrenalin buzz we received from weekly forays into the white plastic future of television series such as *UFO* or *Space 1999*. And we share similar, albeit postdated, memories of the moulded chairs and tube rooms commissioned by Stanley Kubrick for *2001: A Space Odyssey* – elements that we combined to create the ultimate 1970s fantasy room. For us, however, the realities of the Seventies are choppers, space hoppers and *The Multi-coloured Swap Shop*, when people either smelt of sweat or Hai Karate and we caught buses home for 2p.

Chris is already a collector of the period, helped by his mother who trawls car-boot sales and second-hand shops for anything she thinks he might like, and he requires a space in which to display his budding collection. He wants an environment into which his items will fit comfortably, rather than being shriekingly out of place, and his vision is of a fabulously sophisticated early Seventies dining room. This fantasy may seem dangerously necrophiliac to those who remember the period, but although there was a

lot of dodgy design in the era of flares and Afghan coats there were also richly coloured, highly stylized rooms laden with glamour.

Aptly for Chris's dining room fantasy, the 1970s was the period that reinvented the dinner party, when cheese fondue and straw-wrapped Chianti flowed like a mighty river from the glossy white plastic dining tables of the legion of young married hipsters. Aptly, too, for the location of his room – it is basically a transitional space between the living room, kitchen and staircase – he feels that his fantasy is best contained out of sight and out of mind, accessible only on those days when he can really enjoy and appreciate an up-tempo disco beat.

EXPERTS & HELPERS

ANGELA SYKES
CHRIS'S MOTHER

Chris is quick to admit that his mother has had an enormous influence on him. She continues to feed his Seventies obsession and it was she who originally suggested he should buy his 1971 camper van. Angela reminisces about her days dancing in cages in the Sixties and Seventies, in a Manchester club called Jigsaw, wearing hot pants and white plastic knee-high boots. She loved the colour and, although she had initially been concerned that the room might end up looking trashy, thought it very tasteful, sophisticated and grown up. She particularly liked the fake Warhol but couldn't be persuaded to call the purple walls 'aubergine'.

The Bean Bag – synonymous with the Seventies' ethos of comfort.

SEVENTIES DINING ROOM

MY FIRST REACTION TO THE SPACE

At some stage in the mid- to late twentieth century the dining room, like other rooms in the house, had been stripped of any inconvenient period features such as cornices and skirtings, paving the way for a design scheme heavily inspired by the optimistically futuristic design in Gerry Anderson's *Thunderbirds*, with more than a passing nod to the grown-up glamour of Biba.

When I originally surveyed the neat, high, almost square room there was nothing to latch on to, nothing to work around, nothing to bring to the fore, nothing to embellish. There was only one element I wanted to keep: the word DESIRE painted on the wall. Chris's fantasy is different to others in this book because most of us lived through the era that inspired it – and, for me, bringing his vision to life was very much about the desire to return to an adult world that I had experienced as a child. So DESIRE would stay. Everything else would start from scratch. And I knew what 'everything' meant. I knew that we needed curves. More than that, we needed white plastic curves. We needed smoked glass and shag pile. And beyond all that we needed an orange fondue set and a lake of Chianti.

Because the dining room is the main thoroughfare from the front of the house to the back I had to keep access clear for ease of movement. So I decided to create an integrated seating and dining unit which flowed in a series of curved spirals around a central smoked-glass pivot, in the corner below DESIRE. This fitted in with Chris's passion for Seventies curves and helped to define the ergonomics as well as the aesthetics of the space. I wanted to include provision for as many functions as possible in the unit – that *Jim'll Fix It* chair has a lot to answer for – so comfortable elements had to be balanced by efficient storage and elegant lighting.

Chris was keen on a colour scheme of bitter chocolates, *café au laits* and cappuccino spiced up with a bit of orange. I simply couldn't bring myself to do brown, but gave him aubergine as a fallback option, which he fell upon with glee. This could have overpowered the room in a cloud of blackish purple. To lighten

the scheme I faded the aubergine wall and ceiling colour to white at skirting-board level and stained the existing parquet flooring glossy white to reflect the available daylight. All the furniture in the room had to be white and shiny for the same reason. The rather box-like proportions of the room took large, silver stripes on the walls very well. I deliberately knocked off their right-angled corners and added smaller stripes to give a feeling of movement (that *Swap Shop* logo again). The stripes fitted well with DESIRE, which was repainted in a suitably disco font.

I was pleased with the finished effect. It spoke of everything that I loved about the Seventies: Jason King, *Top of the Pops* album covers, Imperial Leather advertisements, Joan Collins's cleavage liberally dowsed in dry Martini by the maladroit Leonard Rossiter. It was a bit like discovering Shangri-la. So far as I was concerned, the decadence of the exercise was all-encompassing. I had created an interior that had absolutely no forward-looking impetus. Everything about it was conceived to create a time tunnel back to 1973.

EXPERTS & HELPERS

MICHAEL TRAINER CAFE POP AND POP BOUTIQUE

In our search for inspiration on the seventies theme, we visited Cafe Pop and Pop Boutique which opened five years ago in Manchester as a showcase for post-war art and design. The boutique sells original 1950s, 1960s and 1970s clothes, furniture and accessories. Michael is in charge of the furniture and accessories and his collection includes a bamboo bar, juke boxes and a brown Draylon-fur bed with built-in radio and stereo. Michael has been collecting Seventies paraphernalia for many years and is very knowledgeable about the period.

SEVENTIES
DININGROOM
THEPROJECTS

'We needed white plastic *curves*, smoked glass and shag pile.'

FLOOR TREATMENT

Chris had installed a timber parquet floor when he moved into the house and the pattern of oblong blocks at right angles to each other was highly redolent of the Seventies. I knew the floor had to be white to maximize the amount of reflected daylight and illuminate the dark colours in the room. Chris was keen that the texture of the wood should still come through.

- I sanded the floor with a disc floor-sander to remove any traces of wax or varnish and prepare the grain of the timber for the next treatment.

- Working in areas approximately a metre square, I painted water straight on to the floor with a large emulsion brush to open up the grain of the timber.

- I applied a rough coat of white acrylic floor paint to the wet area and rubbed it in with a soft cloth to force the paint into the grain. I repeated the process to get the right effect, then applied two coats of heavy-duty gloss acrylic floor varnish. The surface was the perfect counterpoint to the soft white shag-pile rugs that I fixed in place with FoamMount.

YOU WILL NEED:

Disc floor-sander
Water
Large emulsion
    brush
Acrylic floor paint:
    white
Soft cloths
Heavy-duty gloss
    acrylic floor
    varnish
White shag-pile
    rugs
FoamMount

WALL COLOUR

Those impossibly unflattering skintight, long-sleeved Seventies T-shirts, that started off muddy cream and ended up a Ribena-stain purple, sprang to the forefront of my mind as a way around the rather oppressive qualities generated by a black-purple room.

- I painted the walls purple, then chose the lightest shade of the original colour on the colour chart.

- Following the manufacturer's instructions I diluted the paint with water to a consistency suitable for use with a spray gun and sprayed a soft band of light purple on the walls, starting at the level of the top of the curved seating unit and working downwards for about 20cm (8in). This is reasonably easy to achieve by eye alone, although you could mark the right height with a spirit level and feint pencil line.

- I cleaned the spray gun thoroughly, diluted white emulsion with water and sprayed another band between the soft pale purple and the skirting board.

- I used undiluted white emulsion to make a flat plane of white where the soft white band met the skirting board.

ORIANA FIELDING-BANKS
FURNITURE DESIGNER

Oriana has been designing furniture for five years and runs a company called Pure Contemporary Design. She designed a 'Boom' coffee /sideboard table using the contrasting curves and ovoid shapes of the curved seating unit as a starting point.

YOU WILL NEED:

Matt emulsion
paints: dark
purple; light
purple; white
Painter's brush
Water
Spray gun
Spirit level and
pencil (optional)

YOU WILL NEED:

Long spirit level
Pencil
Tape measure
Flat, round object
   such as the lid
   of a paint tin
Low-tack masking
   tape
Acrylic silver paint
Paint brush
Artist's brush

WALL STRIPES

At the end of the Nineties we're used to seeing hand-painted vertical stripes or regularly spaced horizontal bands. In the Seventies, however, architects and designers were adventurous with the wall treatments they specified for their clients. Lines shot off in all sorts of directions, often without the use of a right angle. To get an impression of Starsky and Hutch-like speed, you just need to look at cars of the period with their feature stripes or tram lines.

- When the curved seating unit was in place I decided where I wanted to put the stripes and where they would be used to emphasize some shapes or to blur elements like ceiling junctions and right-angled corners.

- I started to mark the stripes with a long spirit level, pencil and tape measure. I felt very much like going to town with the ones around the seating unit, so when I had marked out the broad bands I added two slimmer stripes to give a feeling of speed.

- To soften the right-angled corners where the stripes changed direction I drew the lines around the lid of a paint tin.

- I masked both edges of the stripes with low-tack masking tape, then painted them with highly opaque acrylic silver paint. Unfortunately, there was no short cut to filling in the curved corners as masking tape won't do curves. I had to paint them carefully by hand and eye, with a good-quality artist's brush.

YOU WILL NEED:

Word in the
    typeface of your
    choice
Paper
Piece of chalk
Low-tack masking
    tape
Pencil
Silver paint
Acrylic flow
    medium
Signwriter's brush
Mahlstick, made
    from a stick with
    cotton wool and
    a cloth taped to
    the end

DESIRE

John Simpson, a local signwriter, came up with a new incarnation for the word DESIRE, based on a book of typefaces that he always keeps by his side. Signwriting is a specialized trade and the brushes that are used have long bristles, far longer than those of artists' brushes so that as much paint as possible can be held on the brush. This allows the signwriter to paint long, uninterrupted lines. Traditional signwriting paints were oil-based enamels that flow easily and cover well but take a long time to dry. Acrylic or emulsion paints can be used. Adding acrylic flow medium makes paint smoother and more 'oily' so that it is easier to 'draw' long lines.

- John drew desire freehand on a piece of paper – if you wish you could use a photocopier to enlarge your chosen word to the required size – then rubbed the back of the paper with chalk.

- He attached the paper, chalk-side down, to the wall with low-tack masking tape and traced the letters line for line with a hard pencil, checking every now and again that the chalk had been adequately transferred to the wall.

- When desire had been chalked on to the wall he mixed silver paint with a little flow medium and painted in the letters. He used a mahlstick to steady and support his hand while he worked.

THE CIRCULAR SHAPES

While adults quaffed dry Martinis, ate stuffed olives and listened to Burt Bacharach hits played on a Hammond organ, kids in nylon tank tops sat watching Lesley Judd wrestle with sticky back plastic on *Blue Peter*. In those days sticky back plastic, or SBP, was a law unto itself and seemed to stick only unto itself. These days, courtesy of late Nineties technological breakthroughs, it is easy to use.

When I saw the seating unit in its naked MDF state, I knew there was only one thing to draw attention to those sexy, sinuous curves: glossy white SBP. It was a risky design decision – I had images of bubbles and wrinkles unhelpfully catching the light along those beautifully executed circular shapes. In fact, applying it was simple.

- I filled a plant sprayer with water and sprayed the area of MDF that I wanted to cover.

- I then unrolled the SBP, cut it to an appropriate length and peeled the backing paper halfway off. The damp surface allowed me to move the SBP around until it was in the right position.

- When it was in place I smoothed it, rubbed it and caressed it until it was flat and all the wrinkles and bubbles had gone.

- The water evaporated after about ten minutes, leaving a durable, wipe-clean and highly sexy surface. I cut away the excess SBP with a scalpel.

YOU WILL NEED:

Plant sprayer
Water
SBP
Scalpel

FANTASY ROOMS

CURVED SEATING UNIT

It was essential to get the right kind of flowing, curving lines for the seating unit. I had originally planned to use flexible plywood or hardboard to face its front, but Frank pointed out that neither would achieve the 'roller coaster' curve I had specified since neither are flexible enough to turn corners at breakneck speed. Even if they made the curve without splitting, the unit as a whole would be inherently weak. So Frank suggested a relatively new product: flexible MDF. Basically the same as standard MDF, but with routs taken out of the back at small, regular intervals, it has all the solid durability of MDF but the routs allow it to bend around even the most complicated shapes.

- I asked Frank to cut a series of shapes out of standard 18mm (¾in) MDF. These effectively constituted the top and bottom of the curve for the seating unit.

- He cut 5 x 5cm (2 x 2in) timber battens to the height of the unit and made a studwork frame, then screwed the MDF shapes and frame together to make a firm 'skeleton'.

- He fixed flexible MDF to the studwork frame with a nail gun. This allowed him to work

quickly around the unit without the added time and labour of screwing the MDF to each batten.

- He used a bull-nosed routing bit to rout the outside edge of the top surface of the unit in a soft and very sexy profile.

- I spray primed the seating unit and, once the primer was thoroughly dry, painted the unit with several coats of white metallized paint, allowing it to dry between coats.

YOU WILL NEED:

18mm (¾in) MDF
5 x 5cm (2 x 2in)
   timber battens
Screws
Flexible MDF
Nail gun and nails
Bull-nosed router
Spray primer
Metallized paint:
   white

BEAN BAG

To make the integrated sitting/living /dining unit suitably comfortable, suitably elegantly slouch-worthy, I wanted a large and admittedly cumbersome crescent-shaped bean bag. This was, without doubt, one of the great comedy moments of the television series. Not only was the bean bag cumbersome, not only was it crescent shaped, it was also in chocolate brown stretch suede. As we stuffed it with polystyrene beads, the more sophisticated onlookers remarked on its similarity to a giant sausage, the less sophisticated – well, it's obvious what they thought.

- I used inexpensive wallpaper lining paper to make an exact template of the curve of the seating unit.

- I used the template to make a sausage-shaped liner, with a zip in one of the external seams, out of heavy-duty canvas. The sausage was filled to bursting point with polystyrene beads and the zip was closed.

- I based a stretch suede cover on the template but made the cover 5cm (2in) smaller all round. Reducing its size helps to keep the shape rigid and stops the bean bag becoming too squashy. The cover was left open at one end.

- The sausage was squeezed into the cover and the open end sewn up. I have to say that the finished object was blissfully comfortable.

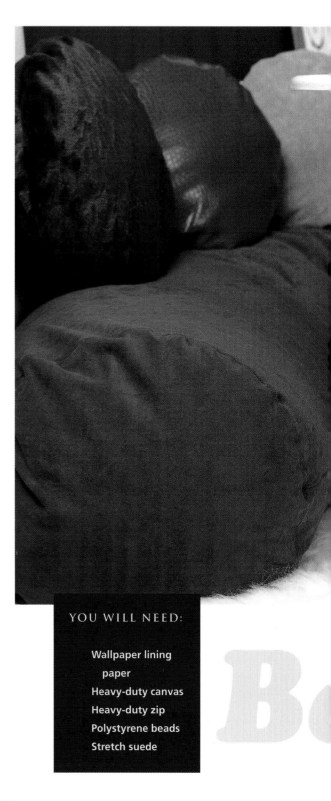

YOU WILL NEED:

Wallpaper lining
    paper
Heavy-duty canvas
Heavy-duty zip
Polystyrene beads
Stretch suede

ANNIE CARMICHAEL
LEATHER CRAFTSWOMAN

Originally from New Zealand, Annie trained as a saddler and learnt traditional stitchwork techniques and how to work with different types of leather. She demonstrated a mixture of hand- and machine-stitching and made three circular cushions in patchwork leather for the curved seating unit. We all agreed that they reminded us of Seventies' waistcoats or handbags.

CUSHION COVERS

I loved the idea of a herd of circular scatter cushions softening the line of the seating unit and raided every available fabric shop for a selection of fake furs, fake suedes, fake lizards and even mock-croc.

I had these made into simple cushion covers for 40cm (15in) diameter cushion pads. I was particularly impressed by the ingenuity of the envelope backs which did away with the necessity for zips, buttons or Velcro. Basically, the back of the cover consists of two pieces of fabric, one of which overlaps the other leaving an accessible gap through which you can (albeit with some fervour), insert the pad.

147

WINDOW HANGING

Net curtains, although very much a Seventies reality, are not part of the Seventies fantasy. The large window in Chris's room did not need a curtain but it did require something to filter the light and also to create privacy since the back of the house is on a public alleyway. In the late 1960s the French couturier André Courrèges designed space age minidresses made from plates of Perspex and these inspired me to create a floor-to-ceiling hanging that covered not only the window but also the radiator below it.

I had the Perspex plates fretcut commercially but cutting and drilling them is not difficult. It is time-consuming, however, although with a bit of patience a small window could receive the same treatment. You would need a fine jigsaw blade to cut the Perspex, a sharp drill bit for the holes, and an electric sander to tidy up the rough edges.

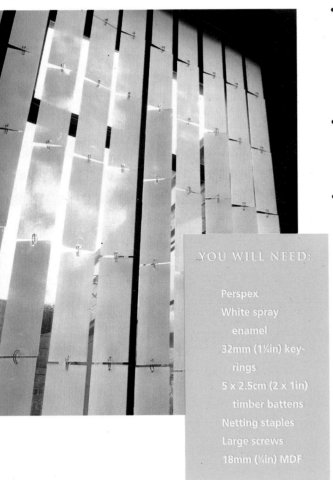

- Perspex was fretcut into 10 x 5cm (4 x 2in) plates with holes at the tops and bottoms and I sprayed the backs of the plates with a fine, slightly blotchy coat of easy-to-use white spray enamel.

- When the enamel was completely dry I linked the plates together with key-rings to make long strands.

- I fixed the key-ring at the top of each strand to a timber batten with a netting staple (imagine a double-ended nail bent into a U), then screwed the batten into the ceiling joists behind a simple pelmet which Frank had made from MDF.

YOU WILL NEED:

Perspex
White spray
enamel
32mm (1¼in) key-
rings
5 x 2.5cm (2 x 1in)
timber battens
Netting staples
Large screws
18mm (¾in) MDF

WARHOL STYLE PORTRAIT

Chris had fallen in love with a multiple portrait of Andy Warhol, executed in typically Warhol style, and a big, brightly coloured art piece was just what I needed to bring more colour into the room.

YOU WILL NEED:

18mm (¾in) MDF
Jigsaw
Spray adhesive
Matt emulsion:
   white
Photograph
Correcting fluid
Acetate
Artist's acrylic
   paints in bright
   colours
Artist's brush
Plain white paper
White cardboard

- My first step was to design a suitably architectural setting for the 'Warhol'. I put two squares of 18mm (¾in) MDF on top of each other and cut out four windows with a jigsaw. I then increased the size of the windows on one of the squares by 1.5cm (½in) all round and glued this square on top of the other one so that the frames were stepped. I painted the MDF with white emulsion.

- I took photographs of Chris pulling a multitude of silly faces then photocopied the best one in black and white and enlarged it to A4. I specifically wanted a poor-quality photocopy that was just dark shadow and as much white as possible. I used correcting fluid to get rid of unwanted midtones and when I was happy with the final result I had four copies of the image transferred to acetate.

- Using a vibrant palette of primary coloured acrylic paints, I splodged colour more or less randomly on to the back of each image with an artist's brush. While the paints were still wet I squashed each sheet of acetate, paint-side down, on to a piece of white paper. The acrylic paint, when dry, is gluey enough to hold the acetate to the paper. I used a spray adhesive to glue the paper on to white cardboard squares that had been cut to fit the spaces in the MDF, put the cardboard squares into the frames – and hey presto, a 'Warhol'. The success of this technique is based on the fact that, like the original Warhol, the black outline of the face is superimposed on bright areas of colour.

THE PRODUCTS

I used the following products for the Seventies dining room.

FLOOR TREATMENT
Disc floor-sander. Hired from HSS
Beckers Aquafloor paint: white. Ray Munn
Beckers Aquafloor Klarlack floor varnish. Ray Munn
White shag-pile carpets. Argos
3M FoamMount. DIY stores; art shops

WALL COLOUR
Dulux matt emulsion: dark purple (74RR 06/129); light purple (30YR 49/097); Brilliant White
Paint spray gun. Hired from HSS

WALL STRIPES
Long spirit level. DIY stores
Easimask low-tack masking tape. Brewers
Formax Mighty metallics silver emulsion paint. Ray Munn

DESIRE
Easimask low-tack masking tape. Brewers
Formax Mighty metallics silver emulsion paint. Ray Munn
Liquetex Acrylic flow medium. London Graphic Centre
Signwriter's brush. Art shops

THE CIRCULAR SHAPES
Crown sticky back vinyl: white (001). Crown Wallcoverings
Scalpel. Art shops

CURVED SEATING UNIT
18mm (¾in) MDF. Jewson
5 x 5cm (2 x 2in) timber battens. Jewson
Flexible MDF. Neatform
Silverman Nail gun. Hired from HSS
Router. Hired from HSS
Zinsser BIN primer sealer. Ray Munn
Hammerite metallized paint: Smooth White. DIY stores

BEAN BAG
Wallpaper lining paper. DIY stores
Heavy-duty canvas. Wolfin Textiles
Heavy-duty zip. John Lewis
Polystyrene bean bag filling. John Lewis
Brown stretch suede. The Cloth House

WINDOW HANGING
Perspex. Jali
Plasti-Kote Super White Spray Enamel. DIY stores
32mm (1¼in) key-rings. Office suppliers
5 x 2.5cm (2 x 1in) timber battens. Jewson
Netting staples. DIY stores
18mm (¾in) MDF. Jewson

WARHOL STYLE PORTRAIT
18mm (¾in) MDF. Jewson
3M Spraymount. Stationers; London Graphic Centre
Dulux matt emulsion: Brilliant White
Artist's acrylic colours: cadmium orange; scarlet; titanium white; emerald green; lemon yellow; purple; violet; ultramarine. Daler Rowney

GENERAL
Kimsta chair. IKEA
Original Seventies plastic lampshade. Pop Boutique
White ceramic vases. Next Home catalogue
Wall Paper magazine. Newsagents
Toughened 6mm (¼in) smoked glass with polished edges, cut to size (70cm/27½in) diameter. Express Glaze
Chrome door handles. Do It All.
Wooden bead curtain. Umaka Gift Shop
Barbara lamp. Habitat
Chrome candlesticks. Ikea
Nugget lamps. Light Concept

CHAPTER 6 ART
NOUVEAU

BEDROOM

Most of us associate Art Nouveau with indulgence. It's a champagne style, a design movement propelled by chocolate truffles and illicit sexual encounters. At the end of the nineteenth century art, literature, music and dance came together in scintillating, showy-offy, sexy spectacles that delighted the eye. Art Nouveau inspired interiors that felt like jewel boxes, made with rich materials brought together for a consciously decadent effect which reflected the *fin de siècle* society that gave birth to the movement. Aubrey Beardsley, Alphonse Mucha et al. created an aesthetic mirror to this louche society, and it is Mucha who inspired Jenna Roberts' vision of an Art Nouveau bedroom.

ART NOUVEAU

What is it about Art Nouveau that makes the sap rise? I can't think of another design style that causes such violent feelings – either ecstatic love or bitter revulsion. One hundred years, almost to the day, since the movement first burst upon the world people's reactions are as emphatically split as they were the first time around.

Art Nouveau happened almost overnight. This must have been one of the most shocking things about it, coming as it did at the end of the aesthetically slow-moving nineteenth century. Not only did it spring fully formed on to an unsuspecting world, it seemed to have come from nowhere. The Arts and Crafts Movement, the flavour of the previous decades, had a reasonable and slow gestation, growing logically from the social changes and Gothic inspirations of the 1850s and 1860s. Suddenly, however, in the 1890s, a new art and design form set Europe alight.

The pace of society had slipped quietly into a higher gear in the middle of the nineteenth century. Manufacturing capability and technical advance, nurtured by the industrial revolution of the mid to late eighteenth century, had its apotheosis in the self-confident, self-advertising Great Exhibition of 1851. Great Britain wanted to show off. And show off she did, with a vast range of over-upholstered, over-indulgent objects that were deliberately pitted against the best the known world had to offer. All the world came to the Crystal Palace in Hyde Park, but not everyone in the world approved of what the exhibition stood for. As in any society, dissenters abounded. And as is so often the case, those who approved the least were the intellectuals, the artists and the young-blade designers of the day. John Ruskin, William Morris, Dante Gabriel Rossetti and the Pre-Raphaelite Brotherhood found the ostentatious vulgarity and mass-produced

Llewelyn-Bowen Art Nouveau at full throttle for Jenna's bedroom.

154

values of the furniture at odds with their cherished socialist views and desire for simplicity and sincerity in all things artistic.

The alternative aesthetic society began producing and marketing a different sort of design: the Arts and Crafts Movement revelled in workmanship, high-quality craftsmanship and a rather rose-tinted utopian view of the sanctity of good, honest labour. Their principal inspiration was the simplistic and solid model of the late Gothic period to which they added a dash of oriental spice derived from the exotic merchandise being imported from Japan whose trade barriers had only recently been lifted. To begin with, the movement came up with rather plain, didactic objects that allowed its customers to live in an idealized fantasy that harked back to a fictional, fairer, rural past.

As the movement developed momentum the Japanese influence moved further to the fore, to the delight of dandies and aesthetes such as Oscar Wilde, publisher Arthur Symons and, of course, the Aesthetic Movement's chief sales representative, the original Mr Liberty. Meanwhile, mainstream taste of the day remained bogged down in successive Louis revivals that ultimately merged with Arabic and Queen Anne influences to create a rich and strangely Moorish style.

But something was about to happen. Late one night a pale, sickly young clerk from Brighton accidentally allowed his ink-dipped pen to slip into the most extraordinary and original shape. Poor thing – his love for line, his passion for illustration knew no bounds, yet it was only in the stolen night-time hours that he could indulge his fantasy. By day he was chained

'Woman as whiplash' - the cradle of Art Nouveau. (Salome *by Aubrey Beardsley.)*

to a desk, by candlelight he illustrated Sir Thomas Malory's *Le Morte d'Arthur* with an extraordinary flattened style that owed everything to Morris, Edward Burne-Jones, Raphael and Boucher, but to which he added a deferential nod to the great Japanese masters such as Hokusai and Utamaro. His nascent talents had brought him into the fast, sexy and androgynous sphere of the latter phase of the Aesthetic Movement, creating one of the greatest literary couplings of modern times: in 1894 Oscar Wilde's *Salome*, with drawings by Aubrey Beardsley, was published.

Beardsley's unique plates showed Wilde's anti-heroine in a variety of

A 1900 Art Nouveau interior by Georges du Feure.

exaggerated, decadent and often masturbatory settings and poses. And on every page, within every vignette, across the frontispiece, the endpapers and even the cover, there is a line that had never existed before: the whiplash. There is a curve in most Japanese woodcuts, there is a flowing grapevine in most Morris wallpapers. The tense curlicue was universally utilized to link shells, monkeys and baskets of fruit in rococo carving. But the bastard child of these elements, the synthesis of all of them, was Aubrey Beardsley's whiplash line. And Europe went mad. In Belgium Victor Horta saw how a whiplash in tensile steel could support a glass roof. In Paris Hector Guimard used whiplashes as the portals for his new entrances to Metro stations. Emile Gallé allowed his enamel glazes to dribble a whiplash and Louis Tiffany introduced the whiplash to America in his great, gaudy glass confections. Within months, a graphic element that had originated from the shuddering hand of a dying youth had united the aesthetic world in a frenzy of entirely original, curvaceous, sinuous, sensuous design.

The Victoria and Albert Museum gave the new movement instant credibility. This august institution had been established soon after the exhibition of 1851 to house examples of artistic and aesthetic endeavour from all around the world that had been shown in the Crystal Palace. Smaller collections of historical and ethnic decorative objects had been added to this nucleus and the museum contained dazzling examples of Morris, Gothic, rococo, Japanese, Javanese and Celtic applied art. So everyone came to study, to refine. For the first (and arguably the last) time, the world knelt in deference at the aesthetic feet of the British – and worshipped.

We British are a queer, moody race. We never seem to recognize our own talents and we certainly seem to be incapable of exploiting them. There we literally were, on top of the world, and yet how many public buildings were commissioned in the new

style? How many underground stations got the whiplash? How many private houses grew tumbling organic tendrils or asymmetric pergolas? None.

OK, so we sexed up arts and crafts a bit. We grafted richer materials on to squat Gothic furniture and we sometimes allowed hinges and lockplates to *almost* undulate, but we hated Art Nouveau. It was too self-confident, too sexual, too unusual and, strangest of all, we actually believed it to be too continental – even though it was described by the French as 'the English style'.

You have to feel sexy to create Art Nouveau. You have to have the time to indulge the line. You have to be able to abstract each element until it can be abstracted no more. Every centimetre of Art Nouveau should be capable of transmuting from animal to vegetable form at a millimetre's notice. Successful Art Nouveau, springing as it does from both groin and brain in equal measure, is difficult to achieve because its original exponents were so incredibly well read. They spent many years studying comparative aesthetic cultures (thanks again to the V & A). They knew that while asymmetry must not mirror itself it must remain perfectly balanced, with equal weight on both sides. And ultimately they knew they had to retain total confidence in their own originality.

Art Nouveau is redolent of the non-stop celebration that we associate with the end of the nineteenth century. And as the twentieth century ends, the style has become a totemic rallying point for all of us who really want to party. When the grey, grey world of reality falls far short of fantasy, the curls and swirls, the animal, vegetable and mineral forms and the all-pervasive whiff of hedonism that is Art Nouveau gets pulled out of the closet for reappraisal.

A fantasy for an Art Nouveau room is a contradiction in terms – any Art Nouveau room is a fantasy room. Oh, and by the way, in case you really haven't sussed it yet, '*j'adore l'Art Nouveau*'.

EXPERTS & HELPERS

PAUL GREENHALGH DIRECTOR OF RESEARCH: VICTORIA AND ALBERT MUSEUM

Paul is an expert on Art Nouveau and is the main curator for the Victoria and Albert 2000 exhibition. Paul guided Jenna and me through the museum's extensive Art Nouveau collection and provided us with an historical perspective on the movement. He was certainly impressed by our fantasy room, and particularly enthusiastic about the colour scheme, but did point out that in the purist *fin de siècle* sense Art Nouveau was incredibly intrusive architecturally. Horta, Guimard and company built rooms from scratch which allowed them complete control over proportions and detailing and gave them the opportunity to create a space that had a radically organic feel.

JENNA ROBERTS
AND HER VISION

Jenna Roberts, her husband Andy and their two small boys, Lewis and Tyler, live in Blackpool. Jenna loves do-it-yourself and together with her mother, who lives close by, has taken on all the decoration of the house – with no help from Andy, whose skills leave a lot to be desired except in the kitchen where he indulges his culinary fantasies with the panache of a masterchef.

Jenna's way into Art Nouveau was through an enthusiasm for the graphic talents of the artist Alphonse Mucha. A Czech working in Paris, Mucha took Art Nouveau and, if such a thing is possible, made it even sexier. Sarah Bernhardt, the Madonna of her age, trusted only him to sell her and her face (and quite incidentally, her plays) to the Parisian public. Mucha quickly rose to pre-eminence and designed everything from cutlery to calendars, bicycle advertisements to brooches – and all with a whiplash line that not only whipped, not only lashed, but also entangled the viewer in a triffid-like series of hungry tendrils. La Bernhardt and the other beautiful women he captured acted as sultry and languid counterpoints to the orgasmic energy their whiplashed hair or thrusting hips expressed.

Jenna loves Mucha because Mucha loved women, something which struck her for the first time when she came across a book of Mucha postcards

EXPERTS & HELPERS

LINDA WATSON
FASHION EXPERT

Linda has worked in and around fashion design, fashion PR and fashion journalism since she left college in 1987 with a double first in fashion design and fashion history. Fashion is indeed her thing. She is currently writing a book on the history of women's fashion in the twentieth century. With the help of costumiers Angels & Bermans, Linda dressed Jenna as a Mucha lady, in various floaty shifts and gorgeously patterned kimonos, transforming late-twentieth century Jenna into late-nineteenth century Jenna the Muse.

in a charity shop about six years ago. He saw them as sexy, confident divas created from a palette of sinuously minimal lines, each of which celebrated a confident and mature vision of femininity. Post-feminist in her originality, Jenna was drawn to this elegant and sophisticated hymn to her own gender, taken from a time much less uniform than our own, and has made it her quest to find out as much about the artist as she can: his work, his interests and his life. Her passion for Mucha has led her to Paris and Brussels, to exhibitions and art galleries to see the furniture and jewellery he designed.

Jenna seems to have avoided all those Mucha reproduction posters that everyone stuck to their walls in the 1970s. She discovered him at an age when she could really appreciate him and her

To Alphonse Mucha women were sexy, confident divas created from a palette of sinuously, minimal lines.
(Alphonse Mucha, 1897.)

passion for Mucha and Art Nouveau grew strong and tall at a time when everybody else had dismissed *fin de siècle* as absurd and outdated. Jenna loves Art Nouveau. And for Jenna, Mucha *is* Art Nouveau.

Mucha worked as an interior designer as well as the originator of startlingly exotic decorative objects. Applying his graphic style to Jenna's bedroom was therefore not going to be difficult.

MY FIRST REACTION TO THE SPACE

Art Nouveau has always been one of my favourite flavours and I was excited about exploring a style I have loved since my teens. I particularly liked the fact that we were going to seek inspiration from Mucha – an artist I continue to adore. Art

JOHN DITCHFIELD
GLASS-BLOWER

John was trained in the ancient art of glass-blowing by Franco Tofflo, an artist from what is probably the world's most famous home of glass manufacture: the island of Murano, near Venice. With that kind of apprenticeship, it's not surprising that John's pieces are widely collected and valuable. We were lucky enough to be able to watch him blow an Art-Nouveau-inspired vase for Jenna, derived from patterns we saw in the Tiffany glass collection at the Haworth Art Gallery in Accrington. It was also inspired by Persian teardrop vases. These were designed to collect the tears shed by a sultan's harem while he was away. The configuration of the neck meant that the tears would not evaporate and the sultan could check the liquid level on his return to see just how much he had been missed.

Nouveau promoted opulence on a lavish and indulgent scale. Even the muted schemes of Horta relied on expensive marble and glass mosaics or the beautifully detailed craftsmanship required to contort fine polished timber into a series of repeating 'S' bends. Trying to re-create the sculptural luxury of the style was going to be difficult without spending the value of Jenna's entire house on her bedroom.

Added to this was the problem of the room's strong personality. Like most of the houses in the street, *chez* Jenna was solidly built between the wars with a riot of very un-Art Nouveau architectural

detailing. The square bay and coloured glass positioned the windows firmly in the 1930s. The off-centre fireplace and fire surround were typical of a metroland speculative builder so I would have to rely heavily on the keynote emphatic curves of *fin de siècle* style to communicate the Art Nouveau message.

Art Nouveau was practised principally by architects who built a room from scratch and could specify the exact proportions and architectural identity of each space. I felt that one of the most efficient ways of effectively rebuilding the room would be to section off the window bay with a fretwork room divider into which I could inset Perspex painted to inspire comparisons with richly coloured Art Nouveau glass. I could also rebalance the off-centre fireplace by creating two curtained niches which would contain Jenna's existing wardrobes. Beyond that, I realized I would have to rely on decorative elements.

It was obvious to both Jenna and me that her bed was to act as the pivot to the whole spinning, swirling scheme and that the colours and wall treatment should be suitably sympathetic to her collection of brightly coloured Mucha reproductions. Although the Dutch motifs in the stained-glass windows screamed Art Deco rather than Nouveau, we decided to use coloured glass as a principal decorative motif. Glass is perhaps one of the most universally recognized Art Nouveau materials. Beyond that, Jenna's fantasy room had to include as many whiplash lines as it was decent to include – and express all the femininity, sexuality and *joie de vivre* of the opulent Art Nouveau world.

ART NOUVEAU BEDROOM THE PROJECTS

'Jenna's *fantasy room had to* include *as many whiplash* *lines as it was* decent *to include.*

FANTASY ROOMS

WALL TREATMENT

I was inspired by the organic forms common to much of Art Nouveau to create a whiplash-shaped stencil. Rather than having an isolated motif below the coving, I decided to place each whiplash at the top of an elegant 'stalk' – a pattern that is characteristic of the Art Nouveau style. By repeating the stalked design regularly around the room, I knew I could create a feeling of architectural rhythm similar to that provided by panelling.

- I painted the wall with pale blue matt emulsion.

- I cut a stencil of the whiplash motif from stencil card and attached it to the wall with low-tack masking tape.

- Referring to the colour chart, I selected the lightest and darkest shades of the base wall colour and added a blob of flow medium to each to make the emulsion a little less sticky. I then painted around the stencil with an artist's medium-sized brush, trying to visualize where shadows and highlights might occur if the shape was three-dimensional. As this is a relatively complicated technique, I tried it out on a board first.

- To achieve the 'stalk' I used a spirit level to lightly mark vertical lines with a pencil. I laid low-tack masking tape on either side of the lines and painted them with the dark and light shades of blue so that the shadows and highlights corresponded with those established on the whiplash motif.

- I repeated the process for the remaining motifs along the wall.

YOU WILL NEED:

Matt emulsion:
blue (wall
colour) and its
lightest and
darkest shades
Stencil card
Low-tack masking
tape
Acrylic flow
medium
Artist's medium-
sized brush
Spirit level
Pencil

THE CEILING

I found the perfect light fitting and to draw attention to it combined it with a painted circle on the ceiling and an 'Art Nouveau' disc. This added another element of depth to the architecture of the room as well as vociferously communicating the Art Nouveau flavour of the scheme.

- A disc was laser-cut from 12mm (½in) MDF and fretcut to my Art Nouveau design. I painted the disc with magnolia emulsion.

- An electrician connected the central light fitting. I made sure the electricity was turned off, then tied one end of a piece of string to the flex of the fitting and a pencil to the other and used this 'compass' to draw a circle around the light.

- I painted the circle with the blue emulsion I had used for the walls.

- Frank attached 5cm (2in) blocks of timber to the ceiling, just inside the perimeter of the circle, and fixed the fretwork disc to them so that it stood away from the ceiling.

Ceiling

YOU WILL NEED:

Fretwork disc cut
from 12mm (½in)
MDF
Matt emulsion:
magnolia; blue
(wall colour)
Ceiling light
String and pencil
5cm (2in) blocks
cut from a 5 x
2.5cm (2 x 1in)
timber batten

THE PEACOCK
PAINT EFFECT

Art Nouveau designers adored the decadent overtones and sumptuous iridescent colours of peacock feathers. I wanted to bring this kind of richness into the room and chose suitably coloured fabrics for the bed cover and cushions, which set off the throw with its peacock-feather design. Using such strong accent colours in a predominantly pale scheme meant also incorporating the odd flash of peacock in the bedhead and the crescent shape above the mantelpiece to keep the colour proportions balanced.

- Fret-cut crescent shapes for the bedhead and overmantel were laser-cut from 12mm (½in) MDF and routed to create a 'ribbed' surface.

- I added a little acrylic flow medium to teal acrylic paint to slow down its drying time and painted this into the ribs with an artist's brush. I then applied viridian, emerald green and cobalt turquoise acrylic paint straight from their tubes. I put each colour on in a line about 5cm (2in) from the top edge of a rib and faded it into the teal following the shape of the crescent as I went around the bedhead.

- For the finishing touch I wet my brush then dipped it into gold powder and lightly dabbed it into the teal colour to create an iridescent effect.

YOU WILL NEED:
12mm (½in) MDF,
    fretcut and
    routed
Acrylic flow
    medium
Artist's acrylic
    colours: teal;
    viridian;
    emerald green;
    cobalt turquoise
Artist's brush
Gold powder

THE WARDROBES

Rather than make over Jenna's nice but un-Art Nouveau wardrobes, I concealed them behind curtains that matched the colour of the wall. I also repeated the wall motifs in the fretwork pelmets that hid the curtain tracks. This minimized the visual intrusion of the wardrobes and introduced a note of symmetry to the room.

YOU WILL NEED:

Overmantel and pelmets, laser-cut from 12mm (½in) MDF
18mm (¾in) MDF for the wardrobe panels
5 x 2.5cm (2 x 1in) timber battens
Curtain tracks
Velvet, lining and curtain heading

- I designed an extravagantly shaped overmantel and had this and two fretwork pelmets that were identical to the wall motifs laser-cut from 12mm (½in) MDF.

- Frank cut three panels of 18mm (¾in) MDF to the height of the ceiling and a little more than the depth of the wardrobes. He cut one panel to the same depth of the others when fixed to the face of the chimney breast on the right-hand side. He then built two open boxes on either side of the fireplace and attached them to the walls with timber battens. He fixed a fretwork pelmet and curtain track to each box.

- The boxes were positioned so that the flank of the righthand box could be brought into the chimney breast to make the fireplace central to the space between the boxes. When the righthand curtain is opened it reveals a shallow space backed by the chimney breast and then the opening for the wardrobe.

- I linked the two boxes with the overmantel. The wardrobes were installed and I hid them behind blue velvet curtains.

TIFFANY GLASS ROOM-DIVIDER

The shifting colours and sensual patterns of Tiffany glass are so synonymous with Art Nouveau that I felt they had to sneak in somewhere. It is easy to cut Perspex with a jigsaw – but remember to use a fine blade.

EXPERTS & HELPERS

BEVERLY BRYSON GLASS CRAFTSWOMAN

Beverly trained initially as a painter and worked as a fine art photographer before she was introduced to glass-making by a friend. What started out as a hobby has become her profession and she works from her studio in London. She is very knowledgeable about the history of glass-making and the specific techniques Tiffany used, and demonstrated one he invented: the use of copper tape to attach pieces of glass to each other and create the gentle curves of his lampshades. Using copper tape rather than lead means the metal can be kept very thin thereby creating a much richer effect, and using many more pieces of glass.

- I designed a room-divider in suitably Mucha style and had the basic shape cut by Frank using a jigsaw from 18mm (¾in) MDF.

- Frank followed my design and cut organic shapes into the room-divider. He then routed some of the shapes and used a jigsaw to cut pieces of Perspex to fit them.

- I used lead on a roll to achieve organic swirly shapes on the front of the Perspex.

- I squirted huge blobs of amethyst, sapphire, Meissen green and turquoise gel glass paints on to the back of the Perspex. A few of the colours contain metallic powders so they sparkled and glittered in the daylight. I also used pink and jade opaline glass paints which have a pearlescent finish. Using several different paints in this way creates a reasonably convincing impression of hand-blown glass.

- I liberally fudged the colours together with a brush and, when I was happy with their position and density, I used the flat of the brush to stipple the paint surface, creating a series of small peaks very like Tiffany glass.

- The paint takes a while to dry, so I waited until the next day then applied an

FRETWORK

The complicated shapes typical of Art Nouveau were often used to create fretwork designs for screens and room dividers. Obviously, a contorted and tricky series of whiplashes would take for ever to cut with a jigsaw. I persuaded Frank to use a power saw for the relatively blocky forms of the room divider, but commissioned a commercial company to use a computer-driven cutter for other, more complicated pieces like the pelmets, ceiling disc and overmantel. This is not a cheap option but does provide consistently high-quality results and you will get more or less exactly what you want in whatever quantities you require.

YOU WILL NEED:

Room-divider
    laser-cut from
    18mm (¾in) MDF
Perspex, cut to
    shape
Jigsaw
Lead on a roll
Gel glass paints:
    amethyst;
    sapphire;
    Meissen green;
    turquoise
Opaline glass
    paints: pink;
    jade
Artist's brush
Strong adhesive
Panel pins

additional coat to make the colours look even richer. Painting the colours on the back of the Perspex means that the lead on the front remains pristine and defined like a stained-glass window.

- I applied a strong adhesive to the Perspex pieces, attached them to the shapes in the room-divider and banged in a few panel pins at an angle to hold them in place. When the adhesive was dry I removed the pins.

171

YOU WILL NEED:

18mm (¾in) MDF
Sandpaper
Copper spray paint
Lining paper
Artist's acrylic
    colours:
    viridian; teal;
    ultramarine;
    emerald;
    turquoise
Gold powder
Artist's brush
PVA adhesive
Mirror glass
Strong glass
    adhesive
Panel pins

MIRROR FRAME

I needed a round shape above the fireplace and as Jenna had no mirror in her bedroom I decided to give her one in a heavy, round frame and kill two birds with one stone. Art Nouveau designers adored the rich effects of semi-precious gems so I devised a fake lapis-lazuli technique.

- Frank cut a frame for the mirror from 18mm (¾in) MDF and I sanded it and then sprayed it with copper paint.

- I cut several large pieces of wallpaper lining paper to the shape of the frame and painted them with random splodges of acrylic paint in rich blue/green/peacock shades. I then sprinkled gold powder into the wet acrylic.

- When the colours were dry I laid one piece of lining paper on top of another and cut them into shard shapes – long, thin wedges like broken china.

- I used a brush to apply PVA adhesive to the frame in a section approximately 30cm (12in) wide and placed 'shards' in the glue while it was still wet. The inside and outside edges of the shards corresponded with the inside and outside of the frame and they fitted closely together like a mosaic in a series of fine wedges, with a quite uniform margin of copper paint showing around each shard.

- When the mosaic was almost dry, I painted a light coat of PVA adhesive straight on to the shards. This helps to flatten the paper and also acts as a varnish or glaze. The adhesive dries clear, so panic not if you seem to be covering up all your hard work under a heavy white coat of glue.

- I repeated the process until I had covered the entire frame with the paper shards. When the frame was completely dry, I attached mirror glass to the back with a strong glass adhesive and held it in place with panel pins which I hammered carefully into the frame. I bent the pins over the glass to keep it secure and removed them when the adhesive had dried.

ART NOUVEAU PEACOCK FEATHER VASE

I was lucky enough to find several copper vases with suitably elegant Art Nouveau proportions, and also the Japanese carved table on which the vase stands, at a market.

YOU WILL NEED:

Vase
Methylated spirits
Enamel sprays:
   teal; blue; green;
   pearlescent
   purple
Peacock feathers

- I wiped the vase with methylated spirits to remove any grease which might prevent the spray paint taking.

- To create a feeling of Art Nouveau enamel I sprayed the vase with teal enamel spray and allowed it to dry thoroughly. I then added blobs of blue enamel and, while this was still tacky, sprayed blobby patches of green around the neck of the vase.

- While the green patches were still wet I did exactly what the instructions on the can tell you not to do, and sprayed a big wet blob of pearlescent purple into the blue areas. This 'separated' the blue paint and allowed the teal undercoat to show through. It also caused the blue to trickle down the vase, taking bits of pearlescent purple with it.

- When the vase was dry I sprayed it lightly with the purple pearlescent spray to get that shimmery, trickly Art Nouveau look and arranged the peacock feathers.

PICTURE FRAME

I couldn't resist having a stab at Mucha style with my pencil drawing of Jenna as a *fin de siècle* vamp. I felt that the pictures in the room had to be framed to suit both the scheme and the contorted curves of her Mucha reproductions and, indeed, her *faux* Mucha-Llewelyn-Bowen. Making an extravagant picture frame and cutting Perspex to size is not difficult and brings pictures within the design of a room.

YOU WILL NEED:

12mm (½in) MDF
Perspex
Hardboard
Matt emulsion:
   magnolia
Picture
Gaffer tape
Scalpel
D-rings and picture
   wire

- I designed a suitably curvaceous shape and had it laser-cut from 12mm (½in) MDF. Perspex and a backing of hardboard were cut to a slightly smaller size than the frame.

- I painted the frame with magnolia emulsion and allowed it to dry.

- I attached the Perspex, picture and backing to the frame with heavy-duty black gaffer tape (which is a major advance on the traditional brown paper stuff that tastes so horrid when you lick it). The back of the frame will never be seen, but be firm with yourself and trim the edges of the gaffer tape with a scalpel.

- I fitted D-rings to the back of the frame and attached picture wire to them.

THE PRODUCTS

I used the following products in the Art Nouveau bedroom.

WALL TREATMENT
Dulux matt emulsion:
  blue. Wall colour 10BB
  56/099; light shade
  10BB 83/017; dark
  shade 10BB 41/113
Stencil card. London
  Graphic Centre
Easimask low-tack
  masking tape. Brewers
Liquitex acrylic flow
  medium. Art shops

THE CEILING
12mm (½in) MDF.
  Jewsons. Fretwork disc
  laser-cut by Jali
Dulux matt emulsion:
  magnolia; blue
  (10BB 56/099)
Ceiling light (638980).
  Homebase
5 x 2.5cm (2 x 1in) timber
  batten. Jewson

THE PEACOCK PAINT
EFFECT
12cm (½in) MDF.
  Fretwork shapes laser-
  cut and routed by Jali
Liquitex acrylic flow
  medium. Art shops
Liquitex acrylic paints:
  real teal (903); viridian
  hue (398); cobalt
  turquoise (169);
  emerald green (450).
  Art shops
Gold powder. Alec Tiranti

THE WARDROBES
12mm (½in) and 18mm
  (¾in) MDF. Jewson.
  Fretwork overmantel
  and pelmets laser-cut
  by Jali
5 x 2.5cm (2 x 1in) timber
  battens
'Swish' curtain tracks.
  Do It All
Velvet. Broadwick Silks
Lining and curtain
  heading. John Lewis

TIFFANY GLASS
ROOM-DIVIDER
18mm (¾in) MDF. Jewson.
  Room-divider laser-cut
  by Jali
Perspex. Homebase
Lead and Light lead on a
  roll. Homebase
Pebeo Gel Crystal glass
  paints: amethyst;
  sapphire; Meissen green;
  turquoise. London
  Graphic Centre
Pebeo Opaline glass
  paints: pink; jade.
  London Graphic Centre
No More Nails.
  DIY stores
Panel pins. DIY stores

MIRROR FRAME
18mm (¾in) MDF. Jewson
Plasti-Kote copper spray
  paint. DIY stores
Lining paper. Homebase
Liquitex acrylic paints:
  real teal (903); viridian
  hue (398); cobalt
  turquoise (169);
  emerald green (450).
  Art shops
Gold powder. Alec Tiranti
PVA adhesive. DIY stores
Mirror glass. Local glazier
No More Nails.
  DIY stores
Panel pins. DIY stores

ART NOUVEAU
PEACOCK FEATHER
VASE
Plasti-Kote enamel sprays:
  teal; blue; harbour
  green, classic purple
  pearl. DIY stores
Peacock feathers.
  Haberdashery shops

PICTURE FRAME
12mm (½in) MDF. Jewson.
  Frame laser-cut by Jali
Perspex. Homebase
Hardboard. Homebase
Dulux matt emulsion:
  magnolia
My own drawing
Gaffer tape. Homebase
Scalpel. Art shops
D-rings and picture wire.
  Homebase

GENERAL
Rug. V&A Enterprises.
  Commissioned from
  Ryalux Carpets from
  Signature Rugs; taken
  from the cover
  illustration by Aubrey
  Beardsley of Sir Thomas
  Malory's *Le Morte
  d'Arthur*
Calico curtains, voile
  curtains. The Original
  Product Company
Bedside lamps. Homebase
Bed. Courts Furnishers
Candles. Prices
Peacock throw. Past Times
Sergio chair. IKEA
Hera fabric. Liberty

ALTERNATIVE DECORATIVE FANTASIES

Fantasy is infinite but space has been limited. So I hope the following ideas will satisfy any fantasists whose particular dream room has not been conceived.

INTERIOR ARCHITECTURE

Changing the shape of a room is one of the most efficient ways of setting the scene for a particular theme – and doesn't have to mean rebuilding it completely.

ROCOCO

ROOM-DIVIDERS

If you refer back to Jenna Roberts' Art Nouveau bedroom, the Mucha-style divider I created was an easily achieved element that altered the look of the room by sectioning off the bay window area. Rooms with bay windows can take a divider very effectively and by changing the shape of the cut-outs you could achieve anything from a Gothic fantasy through to a Moorish or even Baroque one. The shapes are easy to cut and, like the room-divider, could take Perspex cut to size and painted with glass paints. If you are going down the Gothic route, laser-copy

Gothic stained-glass images on to the special transfer paper I used for the images on the walls of the Dan and Sue Shadrake's Roman dining room and transfer them to the Perspex to create your own Pre-Raphaelite heaven.

Draw your design on graph paper first and then mark out a corresponding grid on MDF. I usually like to work on a 1:10 scale, which means that one square on the graph paper corresponds to one square centimetre on the MDF.

WINDOWS

Altering the shape and size of windows as
I did with the round solar disc in Jane
Dunster's Egyptian scheme, or creating fake ones
like the slots on either side of her pylon doorway,
are also good ways of communicating a fantasy or
theme. Here again, Gothic, Moorish or Baroque
arches spring to mind, but you can also think in
terms of Chinese round windows
or even space age amoeba or
futuristic shapes. Anyone
who has a real feel for all
things nautical could use a
series of round windows to
create a maritime theme –
edging the portholes with nice
old-fashioned hemp rope could
lead you down the galleon
route. The possibilities are
almost endless. Arrow slits for medievalists, star shapes for
interplanetary travellers or even windows cut to the perfectly formed
outline of Farrah Fawcett-Major for *Charlie's Angels* fantasists.

A CHINESE WINDOW

ARABIAN OR MOORISH

GOTHIC

chinese window treatment

CEILINGS

More architecturally intrusive projects like lowering the height of the ceiling help to
change the character of any room. The barrel vault in the Egyptian chapter could be
used as the basis for a variety of schemes. Remember that the ceiling can be suspended
and need not actually engage with the walls. For Jane I drilled openings in the vault and
pushed fairy lights through them. An alternative might be to backlight the lowered
ceiling with the existing light fitting.

CREATING SPACE

Using mirror is a great way to make a room more spacious and the dummy mirror
doors on either side of the fireplace in Michelle Renée's Ritz salon created completely

new reflected vistas. The same solution, with a fret-cut shape around the mirror, could lead you down the Gothic path while adding heavier mouldings could help you to create a Baroque palace.

WALL TREATMENTS

Attaching panel mouldings to the wall will give a variety of fantasy effects or, if physically constructing panelling is a bit advanced for your DIY skills, you can fake it with paint.

PANELLING

The timber mouldings I used for the panelling Michelle's largely Louis XVI scheme are available in a variety of styles and would easily work in a Baroque, neoclassical Robert Adam or even Gothic context. Attaching planks rather than mouldings in the same way is a good basis for oriental fantasies such as Chinese, Japanese or even Thai. Make sure the planks are not too thick and therefore not too heavy. Shiplap or tongue-and-groove would be ideal and can easily be attached to the wall with panel pins and a strong adhesive.

PAINTED PANELS

Rococo panels

Imagine using the technique I invented for the Shadrake's Roman ceilings as a wall treatment. Mark out panels with a spirit level, mask them out with low-tack masking tape and paint them in different tones of the same colour. The panels don't necessarily need to be geometric. If you combine this technique with a stencil – I used a whiplash design for the walls in Jenna's Art Nouveau bedroom – you can provide yourself with trompe-l'oeil painted panels appropriate for fantasies like Rococo, Gothic, Chinese, Indian or grand old Baroque.

　　For added sparkle, you could apply gold or silver transfer leaf to the insides of some of the panels, as I did for the solar disc window in the

Thai Panels

Indian Panels

Egyptian chapter. By doing this you could have all of the reflective grandeur of Michelle's Louis-style mirrored doors without going anywhere near a saw or glazier.

HORIZONTAL BANDS

The wall bands in Joni Donoghue's heavenly bedroom made the room seem bigger. Imagine bands of the same depth, but painted in alternating shades of gold and yellow ochre, and you would create a very Moorish atmosphere. Adding texture to the paint – I did this for the walls surrounding Jane's Egyptian bas-reliefs – would heighten the Arabian feel. Horizontal bands in black and white are a strong feature of early Renaissance Florentine buildings and horizontal banding was very popular in the Art Deco period. Richly coloured bands sprinkled with stars and fleur-de-lis are often found in Gothic Revival schemes and are particularly suitable on staircases or in hallways.

If you like the twilight-sky effect of the wall bands in Joni's bedroom and feel brave enough to paint an entire room as a celestial chamber, save time by hiring a paint sprayer to fade the colours as I did on the walls of Chris Sykes' Seventies dining room. For especially twinkly stars spray a 'nimbus' with a mouth diffuser and then silver-leaf a star shape in its centre to both catch and reflect the light – an ideal starting point for *Star Trek*, *Barbarella* or space age fantasies in general.

TEXTURE

Mixing sand and powder filler with emulsion paint to create a stippled texture could be the basis of a Baroque wall treatment that looks like damask or cut velvet. Cut a large,

ALTERNATIVE DECORATIVE FANTASIES

extravagant stencil and apply the textured paint to walls of the same colour. Alternatively reverse the procedure and use shaped 'masks' to create flat patterns on a textured wall, as described in the Egyptian bas-reliefs project.

MARBLED EFFECTS

For a very rich scheme such as Indian, Byzantine or Art Deco, scale up the technique I invented for the Art Nouveau mirror frame. Paint lining paper in rich, splodgy or delicate stone colours and decoupage them on to the wall with PVA adhesive. Pale greys and whites would give the impression of marble blocks if you paint the wall pale grey beforehand. These make an excellent starting point for a variety of fantasies. Using this treatment in conjunction with more richly coloured patterns would allow you to re-create the fabulous marble inlays of the Taj Mahal.

FURNISHINGS

Making your own furnishings and accessories for a dream room can make the fantasy that much more convincing.

FABRICS

The richly patterned borders of saris are an ideal basis for glamorous exotic schemes as well as for more restrained neoclassical fantasies. Saris are often opulently coloured and can be simply draped for maximum impact. Arabian, Baroque or (obviously) Indian fantasies call for heavy draping at a window, around a bed or even to add emphasis to mirrors, pictures or fire surrounds. Be very careful about combining drapes and candles, however. Real opulence junkies might even go so far as to combine patterned silks such as saris with fake fur or crystal edgings.

MIRROR AND PICTURE FRAMES

Cutting MDF into an appropriate shape for a mirror or picture frame is not difficult and, taking Jenna's Art Nouveau picture frame as inspiration, simplified Gothic, Indian, Renaissance or Baroque shapes work well. Products like relief cream or plastic mouldings bring surface detail to otherwise flat shapes. The beauty of making your own

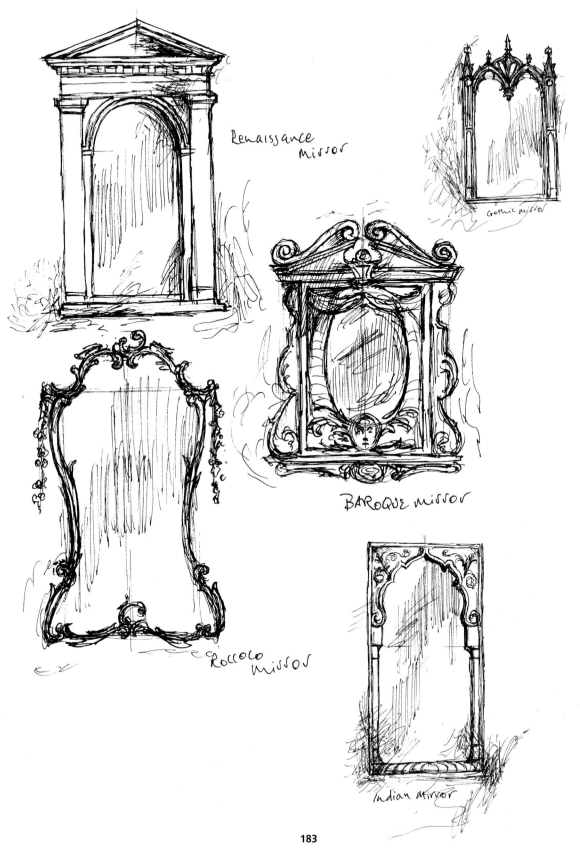

Renaissance Mirror

Gothic mirror

Baroque mirror

Rococo Mirror

Indian Mirror

ALTERNATIVE DECORATIVE FANTASIES

frames is that you can control their scale and size. If you are making a mirror, most glaziers will drill holes in the glass allowing you to attach a candle sconce in front of it so that the candlelight is reflected and magnified.

SURFACE EFFECTS

Space age enthusiasts can take advantage of the seamless white shininess of the sticky back plastic used for the curved seating unit in the Seventies chapter to make space-ship consoles or futuristic furniture. Glossy black SBP could turn a simple pine cupboard into a black lacquer cabinet appropriate to any fantasy from Japanese through Baroque or chinoiserie to Thai.

CHANGING SHAPES

Changing the shape of junk furniture or inexpensive packflats is easy with MDF and wood-glue. The celestial chairs in the heavenly bedroom sprouted angelic wings but could just as easily become Baroque thrones, Gothic chairs or Indian love seats. The simple addition of a headboard to an otherwise unremarkable bed can be a valuable tool in pursuit of a fantasy, and cutting a shape or design into one made from MDF could be used for the headboard of a grand four-poster bed. The technique is the same as

BAROQUE BED MAKE-OVER
USING PAINTED MDF

the one I used for the Art Nouveau room-divider and, as with the divider, Gothic-window shapes or more pointed Moorish arches are easy to cut.

A bed may not necessarily be for sleeping in but could become a sumptuously comfortable day bed piled with cushions and bolsters, as in the Ritz salon. Other great recliners were the Ottomans and, of course, the Romans. Ottoman style is very similar to Arabian or Moorish design and could rely on rich fabrics in jewel colours. For Roman style have a look at the Shadrakes' reincarnated single bed couches.

Indian DAY Bed or Bed treatment

Renaissance day bed

Roccoce

SAFETY

When carrying out any DIY, safety must be considered at all times. Every job that is carried out on *Fantasy Rooms* is checked and double-checked by professionals.

When using any product, it is always important to follow the manufacturer's instructions regarding the use of the product and for your own safety. Remember that when you are using any kind of spray to work in a well-ventilated area and to wear a safety mask to protect yourself. Many products are toxic and may be corrosive, so ensure that you keep yourself, your children and your pets safe from potential harm. If you are cutting, wear protective gloves and goggles or a safety mask.

Electricity can be very dangerous. Always use a qualified electrician to tackle any projects that require complicated wiring and to check any electrical equipment that has recently been installed. Always buy equipment that is correctly earthed and displays the kitemark (the British mark of safety). Never drill or hammer into walls unless you have taken steps to ensure there are no hidden electricity cables or pipes.

Machinery used for DIY projects can also represent a threat. Make sure you do not leave blades and tools where they can be reached by children. Whether you are hiring or buying equipment, be realistic about your capabilities and ensure that you know fully how to use the equipment properly. In the wrong hands, something as simple as an electric drill can be very dangerous.

To make your fantasy real, complicated or dangerous projects must be left to the professionals. Whilst basic instructions are given for completing the projects in the book, you must use your own common sense to protect yourself and your environment from any harm.

PLACES TO VISIT

The following are places we visited as well as useful addresses should
you wish to further an interest in one of the fantasies.

EGYPTIAN DINING ROOM

The British Museum
Great Russell Street
London WC1B 3DG
Tel. 0171 636 1555

The Dulwich
Picture Gallery
(until Jan 2000)
119 Park Hall Road
London SE21 8ES
Tel. 0181 693 5254
(after Jan 2000 back to
old address)
College Road
Dulwich
London SE21 7AD
Tel. Same as above

The Horniman
Museum
100 London Road
Forest Hill
London SE23 3PQ
Tel. 0181 699 1872

The Petrie Museum
UCL
Gower Street
London WC1E 6BT
Tel. 0171 387 7050

HEAVENLY BEDROOM

Chapel of the Guardian
Angels
Winchester Cathedral
5, The Close,
Winchester SO23 9LS
Tel. 01962 853 137

Hampton Court Palace
Surrey KT8 9AV
Tel. 0181 781 9500

The Heaven Room
Burghley House
Stamford
Lincolnshire PE9 3JY
Tel. 01780 752 451

The Hempel Hotel
31-35 Craven Hill
Gardens
London W2 3EA
Tel. 0171 298 9000

The Royal Pavilion
Brighton BN1 1EE
Tel. 01273 290 900

Westminster Abbey
20 Deans Yard
Westminster Abbey
London SW1P 3PA
Tel. 0171 222 5152

ART NOUVEAU BEDROOM

Criterion Brasserie
224 Piccadilly
London W1V 9LB
Tel. 0171 930 0488

The Geffrye Museum
Kingsland Road
London E2 8EA
Tel. 0171 739 9893

The Haworth Art
Gallery and Tiffany
Collection
Manchester Road
Acrington
Lancashire BB5 2JF
Tel. 01254 233 782

The Musée d'Orsay
62 Rue de Lille
Paris 75007
Tel. 33 140 494 814

The Victoria & Albert
Museum
Cromwell Road
London SW7 2RL
Tel. 0171 938 8500

The Victor Horta
Museum
15 Rue de la
Rhetorique
St. Gilles
Brussels
Tel. 32 253 827 42

RITZ SALON

Buckingham Palace
London SW1A 1AA

Hotel de Crillon
10 Place de la Concorde
Paris 75008
France
Tel. 3314 471 1500

The Ritz Hotel
150 Piccadilly
London W1V 9DG
Tel. 0171 493 8181

Spencer House
27 St. James' Place
London SW1A 1NR
Tel. 0171 499 8620

The Victoria & Albert
Museum
Cromwell Road
South Kensington
London SW7 2RL
Tel. 0171 938 8500

The Wallace Collection
Hertford House
Manchester Square
London W1M 6BN
Tel. 0171 935 0687

ROMAN LIVING ROOM

The British Museum
Great Russell Street
London WC1B 3DG
Tel. 0171 636 1555

Colchester Castle
14 Reigate Road
Colchester CO1 1YG
Tel. 01206 282 931

Fishbourne Roman
Palace
Salthill Road
Fishbourne
Chichester
W. Sussex PO19 3QR
Tel. 01243 785 859

Lullingstone
Roman Villa
Stone Lane
Eynsford
Dartford
Kent DA4 0JA
Tel. 01322 863 467

Museum of London
London Wall
EC2Y 5HN
Tel. 0171 600 3699

The Roman Baths &
Amphitheatre
High Street
Caerleon
Newport
Wales NP6 1AE
Tel. 01633 422 518

The Roman Baths
The Pump Room
Stall Street
Bath BA1 1LZ
Tel. 01225 477 784

Roman Legionary
Museum
High Street
Caerleon
Newport
Wales NP18 1AE
Tel. 01633 423 134

SEVENTIES DINING ROOM

The Barbican Centre
Silk Street
Barbican
London EC2Y 8DS
Tel. 0171 638 4141

Design Museum
28 Shad Thames
Butler's Wharf
London SE1 2YD
Tel. 0171 403 6933

Pizza Express
Fulham Road
363 Fulham Road
London SW10 9TN
Tel. 0171 352 5300

Royal National Theatre
Upper Ground
South bank
London SE1 9PX
Tel. 0171 452 3333

The Victoria & Albert
Museum
Cromwell Road
London SW7 2RL
Tel. 0171 938 8500

SUPPLIERS AND STOCKISTS

Amtico Flooring
Company
Head Office
& Factory
Kingfield Road
Coventry CV6 5PL
0800 667766

Angelic
6 Neal Street
London WC2
0171 240 2114

Argos ring and reserve
0870 600 1010

B & Q Plc (Head Office)
Portswood House
1 Hampshire Corporate
Park
Chandlers Ford
Hampshire SO53 3YX
01703 256256

Brewers
327 Putney Bridge Road
London SW15 2PG
0181 788 9335

The British Museum Shop
Great Russell Street
London WC1B 3DG
0171 323 8175

Broadwick Silks
9-11 Broadwick St
London W1V 1FN
0171 734 3320

Café Pop (Pop Boutique)
34/36 Oldham Street
Manchester M4
0161 236 5797

The Carpet Company
Unit 3
118-120 Garratt Lane
London SW18 4DJ
0181 875 1255

China Presentations
1-2 6-7 The Broadway
Forty Avenue / Preston
Road
Wembley
Middlesex HA9 8JT
0181 904 7721

Classic Pot Emporium
30a Straight Road
Boxted
Colchester CO4 5HN
01206 271946

Clayton Munroe Ltd
Kingston West Drive
Kingston Staverton
Totness
Devon TQ9 6AR
01803 762626

The Cloth House
98 Berwick St.
London W1V 3WP
0171 287 1555

ColArt Fine Arts
and Graphics
helpline
0800 212 822

Cornellison
105 Great Russell Street
London WC1B 3RY
0171 636 1045

Courts
Staples Corner
Geron Way
Edgware Road
London NW2 6LW
0181 450 9538

Crown Paints
PO BOX 37
Crown House
Hollins Road
Darwen
Lancashire BB3 0BG
01254 704951

Crown Wallcoverings
Hotline 0800 4581554

Cuckoo Fashions
207 Whitechapel Road
London E1 1DE
0171 247 7950

Daler Rowney
12 Percy Street
London W1A 2BP
0171 636 8241

Do It All
0800 436 436
information line

The Dover Bookshop
18 Earlham Street
London WC2H 9LN
0171 836 2111

Dulux Paints
Dulux Advice Centre
01753 550555

DZD Blyco
Lower Ground Floor
145 Tottenham
Court Road
London W1P 9LL
0171 388 7488

Epra Fabrics Ltd
54 Brick Lane
London E1 6RF
0171 247 1248

Express Glaze
75A Stockport Road
Denton
Manchester M34
0800 371 153

The Fallen Angel
Bookshop
17 Fisher Street
Lewes
BN7 2DG
01273 487 809

Glass Express
56-58 Lupus Street
London SW1 V3EE
0171 828 6046

Homebase Ltd
01923 248511
information line

Homecrafts Direct
PO Box 38
Leicester LE1 9BU
0116 251 3139

HSS Hireshops Plc
143 Caledonian Road
London N1 0SL
0845 728 2828

Ikea Ltd
Ikea Brent Park
2 Drury Way
North Circular Road
NW10 0TH
0181 2085600

Jali
Albion Works
Church Lane
Barham
Canterbury
Kent CT4 6QS
01227 831710

Jewson Ltd
Baltic Sawmills
Carnwath Road
SW6 3DS
0171 736 5511

John Lewis Partnership
278-306 Oxford Street
London W1A 1EX
0171 629 7711

Kalon
Huddersfield Road
Barstall
Batley WF17 9XA
01924 354 5000

Kingsmead Carpets
Caponacre Industrial
Estate
Cumnock
KA18 1SH
01290 421511

Leyland Paints
Head Office
01924 477201

Liberon Waxes Ltd
Mountfield Industrial
Estate
Leeroyd Road
New Romney
Kent TM28 8XU
01797 367555

Liberty Plc
214 Regent Street
London W1R 6AH
0171 734 1234

Light Concept
PO Box 511
Hitchin
Herts SG5 1UY
01462 442941

London Cornice
Company
Unit 3
19 Osiers Road
London SW18
0181 875 9779

London Graphic Centre
16-18 Shelton Street
Covent Garden
London WC2H 9JJ
0171 240 0095

Melrose Textiles
Allerton Mills
Allerton
Bradford BD15 7QX
01274 491277

Nasar Collections
232 Upper Tooting Road
Tooting
London SW17
0181 682 9990

The National
Gallery Shop
Trafalgar Square
London WC2N 5DN
0171 747 2870

Next Home Catalogue
0845 6007000
information line

Office World
0800 500024
mail order and info

Osborne and Little
49 Temperley Road
London SW12 8QE
0181 675 2255

Past Times
155 Regent Street
London W1R 7FD
0171 734 3728

Pentonville Rubber
104-106 Pentonville
Road
London N1 9JB
0171 837 4582

The Pier
200 Tottenham Ct Road
London W1P 0AD
0171 637 7001

Plasti-Kote
London Road
Industrial Estate
Pampisford
Cambridge CB2 4EE
01223 836400

Polyvine Ltd
Vine House
Rockhampton
Berkley
Gloucs GL13 9DT
01454 261276

Prestige Flooring
Systems House
Eastbourne Road
Blindley Heath
Surrey RH7 6JP
01342 832560

Price's Patent
Candle Co. Ltd
110 York Road
London SW11 3RU
0171 228 2001

Ray Munn
861 Fulham Road
London SW6 5HP
0171 736 9876

Relics of Whitney
35 Bridge Street
Whitney
Oxfordshire OX8 6DA
01993 704611

Rosalie Owen
1276 High Road
Whetstone
London N20 9HH
0181 446 5650

VV Rouleaux
54 Sloane Square
London SW1W 8AX
0171 730 3125

Scumble Goosie
Lewiston Mill
Toadsmore Road
Brimscombe
Stryde
Gloucestershire
GL5 2TB
01453 731305

Secret Garden Centre
Westow Street
Upper Norwood
SE19 3AF
0181 771 8200

Shortwood Carvings
8 Gun Wharf
Old Ford Road
London E3 5QB
0181 981 8161

Silverman
(do not supply to the
domestic market but
distribute to timber
yards and will advise)
0181 327 4000

Solar Solutions
Fountains
6 High St
Kington
Herts HR5 3AX
01544 230303

The Stencil Store
20/21 Heronsgate Road
Chorleywood
Herts WD3 5BN
01923 28557788

Stylogue
Shakespeare Way
Whitchurch
Business Park
Whitchurch SY13 1LJ
0870 600 6070

Talisman Trading
Unit 13
Victoria Industrial
Estate
Victoria Road
London W3 6UU
0181 896 1881

Tiranti Alec Ltd
27 Warren Street
London W1P 5DG
0171 636 8565

Travis Perkins
01604 592428
01604 592286

Umaka
5A Walker's Court
London W1R 3FQ
0171 437 5193

Wickes Building
Supplies Ltd
Head Office
120-138 Station Road
Harrow
Middlesex HA1 2QV
0181 901 2000

Winther Browne
Ealy Estate
Nobel Road
Edmonton N18 3DX
0181 803 3434

Wolfin Textiles
64 Great Tichfield Street
Oxford Circus
London W1P 7AE
0171 636 4949

Woolworths PLC
Head Office
242 Marylebone Road
London NW1 6JL
0171 262 1222

Wynchwood Design
Viscount Court
Brize Norton
Oxfordshire OX18 3QQ
01993 851 435

INDEX

Neo-classical

AUTHOR'S ACKNOWLEDGEMENTS

FIRST AND FOREMOST MY FELLOW FANTASISTS:

Peter Bazalgette, Linda Clifford, Caspar Peacock and Susannah Walker,
Liz O'Brien, Vicky Thompson, Dan Dimbleby, Jo Haddock,
Toby Fricker, Nick Gillam-Smith, Tracy Gullen,
Frank the Plank, Dee Shoosmith, Julie Fowler, Jonathan Martin,
Clare Bradley Colin, Chris and the film crews, and Mick who strove to
get me there on time.

WILLIAM HUNT

I thought it was only tactful that I should not clash with any of the
fantasies I created for the series. I am therefore enormously grateful to
William Hunt who ran up a series of fabulous and fantastical outfits
specifically conceived to complement each of the interiors.

He is, without doubt, the only tailor in London who would not blanch at the briefs he was
given – anything from an Egyptian Pharaoh in shades of gold to a Mephistophelean blue silk
ensemble for the heaven programme.

As far as I am concerned, achieving an interior fantasy is only the first step. For all you
fantasists out there, once your room has been done, remember to get the right smell, the
appropriate booze and above all, the perfect outfit to live your fantasy truly.

EXPERTS AND HELPERS

I'm also grateful to the following experts and helpers who contributed to the series:
Felicity Irons, the rush matting expert, who wove an authentic Egyptian-style basket
for our Egyptian dining room; Hugo Bourcier, the Aubusson carpet dealer, who inspired me to
paint my own version of the Aubusson rose on the firescreen in Michelle Renée's Ritz salon;
Maurice, the Tarot card expert, who divined Joni Donoghue's state of mind
and was full of the most extraordinary psychic revelations about the crew; Henry Pocock, the
candle expert, who made some church candles for Joni's bedroom to give it that heavenly, gentle
flickering light; Karin Taylor, the healer who brought a special crystal that brought the energy of
angels to Joni's heavenly bedroom; Sally Grainger, an expert on classical food and professional
chef, who made some Roman takeaway food for us in her flatpack kitchen for the Roman living
room episode; and Peter VcVeigh, the installation artist who runs the Glasgow company Glow:
Design in Light. He made a kinetic light sculpture or 'Dreamlamp', in rich, bitter tangerine
colours for the Seventies living room.